IKE OGUINE is Nigerian is his first novel.

IKE OGUINE

A SQUATTER'S TALE

Heinemann

Heinemann Educational Publishers
Halley Court, Jordan Hill, Oxford OX2 8EJ
A Division of Reed Educational & Professional Publishing Ltd

Heinemann: A Division of Reed Publishing (USA) Inc.
361 Hanover Street, Portsmouth, NH 03801–3912, USA

OXFORD   MELBOURNE   AUCKLAND
JOHANNESBURG   BLANTYRE   GABORONE
IBADAN   PORTSMOUTH (NH) USA   CHICAGO

First published by Heinemann Educational Publishers in 2000

British Library Cataloguing in Publication Data
A catalogue record for this book is available from the British Library.

Library of Congress Cataloging-in-Publication Data
Oguine, Ike
      A squatter's tale
         p.   cm. — (African writers series)
      ISBN 0-435-90655-0
      I. Title. II. Series.
   PR0000.0.000000 2000
   000 — dc21   00-0000
                                    CIP

AFRICAN WRITERS SERIES and CARIBBEAN WRITERS SERIES and
their accompanying logos are trademarks in the United States of America
of Heinemann: A Division of Reed Publishing (USA) Inc.

Cover design by Touchpaper
Cover illustration by Joanna Clinton

Phototypeset by SetSystems Ltd, Saffron Walden, Essex
Printed and bound in Great Britain by
Cox and Wyman Ltd, Reading, Berkshire

ISBN 0 435 90655 0

00 01 02 03 04 10 9 8 7 6 5 4 3 2 1

For O.D.M. and Black Soul

My Uncle Happiness

The most memorable event of the tenth year of my life was the arrival of my Uncle Happiness at our house in Yaba, Lagos, Nigeria on a visit from America. It was his first and, to date, only visit to his home country since he had left in January 1970, claiming to the Americans to be on the run from the Nigerian government which he said had placed him on a Wanted List because of his exploits in the Biafran Army during the just-ended Nigerian civil war. He had, in fact, largely spent the war concealed in the toilet of my parents' house in our hometown, his heart pounding in tune to the real and imagined bootfalls of the Biafran Army's conscripting squads. Uncle Happiness was a huge, perfectly black, perfectly smooth balloon, topped with a black balloon-shaped, clean-shaven head divided in the middle by the widest smile on earth. He was supported by two boomerang legs that did not walk but gently rolled forward, like wheels. That rain-sodden evening in 1976, the balloon was packed into a dark brown cowboy outfit, straight from Hollywood, which included a ten-gallon hat and spurs. The only thing missing was a holstered pistol.

Still clutching four mighty travelling bags, two in each hand, and bellowing directions to a small man behind him on how to ease a mighty trunk past the door of our house, he swept me into his arms as soon as I opened the door. He yelled: 'Obi the Giant! Obi the Giant! Only a tiny ant yesterday! Only a tiny ant!' He also quickly seized my elder sister who had come up behind me: 'Princess, Beautiful Princess, Adaku, Daughter of Wealth! Only an ant yesterday!' My mother, coming from the

1

kitchen to investigate the cause of the commotion, leapt at her only brother, crushing Adaku and me into the squashy stomach of the balloon, adding her own cries: 'My eyes are lying to me! It is not true!' to her brother's: 'Beautiful Woman! Younger every day! Others are going forward, getting older, you are going backwards, getting younger!' My father was not swept up in an embrace when he came downstairs drawn by the noise of rejoicing, probably because in his old shirt and wrapper and reading glasses, a rolled-up newspaper in his hand, his spare, serious frame did not look huggable; but Uncle Happiness did the next best thing: he poured on my father all the praise names imaginable, alluding to his learning, his kindness, his gentleness, his handsomeness, drawing from my father's face a rare coy smile. My younger sister, Nwaka, the youngest of my parents' three children, was only two years old at the time and was safe from my uncle in her bed upstairs. We had not known he was coming because the letter he had written to inform us only reached our mailbox weeks after he had returned to America.

Uncle Happiness, surrounded by his trunk and travelling bags, was so much larger than life that our long living room seemed to shrink around him. He whistled and yelled and bellowed. He cast his eyes towards the ceiling and shouted thanks to the Almighty for bringing him home safely. Then inspired by a *highlife* tune that was playing on the radio, he went into a wild dance of celebration. His hands rotating above his head like windmills, he swung his waist this way and that, pendulum-fashion, then, his left leg raised, he hopped around the living room like an excited baboon. His soft stomach leapt about wildly, struggling to free itself from his cowboy shirt, from his body, pushing oohs, aahs, hohos and hahas out of Uncle Happiness's throat. He stopped suddenly, executed two incredible pirouettes and after that began to shake his buttocks madly. Sweat dropped off his face like tennis balls, a greedy stream soaked his armpits, his back and his waist.

2

The seat of his tight cowboy trousers stretched so taut it seemed about to explode. My mother shook her shoulders to the music, modestly accompanying her brother without abandoning the propriety of an adult; my father looked deeply confused. I, too, was confused: adults, I'd been brought up to believe, always behaved properly, didn't suddenly break into wild dancing, didn't jerk their hips all over the place in a lewd, abandoned manner. When Happiness's celebration finally came to an end, we, the onlookers, were as exhausted as him.

Uncle Happiness's bags and trunk brought for us the sort of fabulous riches you hear about in folk-tales. For me alone there were sets of shirts and pants and shorts and caps and shoes of dazzling colours and styles, different sets of pens, three different school bags, one of his wonderful, shiny travelling bags and, the gift that dwarfed all gifts, that made Adaku look miserably at the brightly flowered clothes and bags he bought for her and eye me dangerously, was a cowboy outfit exactly like the one he wore. In fact, I thought that my own waistcoat (or monkey-jacket as we called it at the time) was even more beautiful than his. My mother got a pile of fabrics which Uncle Happiness said he had ordered specially from Holland, shoes, bags, new pots and pans and a portrait of herself made from an old photograph in which she looked fifteen years younger. For years after, when my mother wanted to taunt my father, she'd tell him that the only new clothes she had were the ones her brother had brought for her from Holland and America donkey years before. My father, who chose his fights very carefully, would smile an embarrassed smile and keep quiet. My father got a small radio that was also a cassette player and a calculator, an electric shaver, half a dozen ties and more than ten bottles of spirits, which he kept locked in a drawer in his bedroom and drank alone with a scowl on his face to keep anyone from asking for a drop. There was loads of baby's things for Nwaka, and for the

3

whole family Uncle Happiness brought monstrous tins of powdered milk and Quaker Oats, cartons of corn flakes and sugar,
and roast turkey and chicken in barbecue sauce wrapped in
aluminium foil and still warm – at least that is how I remember
it – after flying thousands of miles across oceans and deserts. It
remains the best chicken and turkey I've had in my life, and I
remember, whenever a family friend or relative came to the
house that week and my mother yanked off another large chunk
of chicken or turkey for them, feeling as wounded as if she were
cutting and offering up parts of my body.

I was the second man of the house, next only to my father,
and Uncle Happiness gave me special attention. Every morning
he took me on jaunts to Broad Street and the Marina, Bar Beach,
the museum, Federal Palace Hotel, or to visit relatives or to buy
the things he would take back to America. I ate meat pies,
chocolates, buns, cakes, ice cream and all the other wonderful
things my mother had decreed were never to be touched or only
eaten in pitiful quantities at Christmas or at birthday parties. In
our cowboy outfits, which I insisted we wear every day until my
mother put her foot down and said they had to be washed, we
attracted more attention than the shops on the Marina and the
highlife band at Federal Palace. Children, and some adults too,
gathered to stare at us and to exclaim 'Americana' or 'High
Chaparral' or 'John Wayne'; the daring stepped forward and
brushed their fingers across my monkey-jacket as I struggled to
keep pace with my rolling uncle. I was the happiest ten-year-old
in Lagos.

In the evenings, the family gathered around Uncle Happiness
to hear him talk about America.

'The shops, heyiee, one is like from Yaba to Lagos Island, with
everything in this world, you will buy bread and a car from the
same shop. I hear some shops even sell airplanes, I've not seen

4

any like that, but I've been in many shops where you'll be buying matches and behind you are cars on sale. The shops are like towns. No, they are not just like towns, they *are* towns. Twenty thousand people will be shopping together at the same time. More than one hundred cashiers. Their hands fly over the cash machines *kpraa kpraa kpraa* and they tell you how much you are to pay in a second. Some cashiers serve more than ten thousand people in a day.

'The roads, heyiee, those roads, those roads, heyiee, twenty lanes, thirty lanes like football fields made from tar. It will take you twenty minutes or even thirty minutes to walk across some roads. All the cars are new and very fast, no old cars are allowed on the roads.'

Uncle Happiness's eyes would widen in wonder as though each telling renewed, indeed increased, America's dazzle, as though America was so amazing that no matter how long you lived there it continued to astonish, to overwhelm, you.

'The buildings, heyiee, the buildings so tall, so tall. We think we have tall buildings in Lagos, but I tell you no building in Lagos Island is half as tall as the tall buildings in the smallest village in America, the smallest village. There's a building in New York, that building, heyiee, so tall, the Empire House, that's the name, the Empire House. I hear that from that building you can see what is going on in the moon, I hear that when people fly to the moon you can watch them from the top of Empire House, you can even see other countries from there if you have good eyes, not like Nigeria, that is too far away, but neighbouring countries like Canada and Mexico.

'Food, heyiee, the food in that country. They throw food away, food loaded in many lorries. The man whose job it is to throw away the food is one of the richest men in America because he has so much food to throw away and he is very well paid because

5

he does a difficult job. Can you imagine it? A man whose job is throwing food away. If you are walking along the streets, people will be handing food to you from vans just like that.

'America is a land blessed by God,' he would conclude every time, exhaling loudly, left breathless by the great nation beyond the seas.

On the evening Uncle Happiness suggested that you could see the moon and Canada and Mexico from atop the Empire State Building, my father mumbled goodnight to us, picked up his newspaper and went upstairs to his room, after having given my uncle a look of distaste. He never attended any of Uncle Happiness's evening story-tellings after that, preferring to spend the time in his room upstairs reading the papers.

My mother was no gullible fool. She'd attended what in those days was called an advanced teachers' college and had taught in secondary schools for many years before giving up the chalk to run a provisions shop, in spite of my father's objections, believing with remarkable foresight that they could not both put all their eggs in the basket of government monthly wages. But, like Adaku and I and our fourteen-year-old cousin who lived with us at the time, she lapped up every tale Uncle Happiness told and even prodded him with her own grunts of amazement and little shouts at the fantastic things that happened routinely in the land blessed by God. Perhaps she allowed that his enrichment of the bare facts of the things he told about was necessary to convey effectively the magnitude of America's enormous wealth and its miraculous scientific achievements. Or maybe she was just too pleased to see her brother after such a long time, too grateful for the fabrics from Holland to bother about minor things like whether or not it was possible to take a peek at the moon or at Canada from atop the Empire State Building.

Now, when I think back, I realise that even my father's quiet withdrawal from the story-telling was not really in character. He was a compulsive and acerbic arguer even about things he knew next to nothing about and if it hadn't been for the radio that was also a cassette player and also a calculator and Uncle Happiness's other presents, my father would probably have called him a liar to his face.

Adeyemo, our neighbour and landlord, strolled in one evening while Uncle Happiness was serving more fantastic slices of America to us. He had a large, noisy family, a wife and six children, aged between fifteen and twenty-three, and an army of near and distant relations, whom he said bothered him all day. So whenever he could he slipped across the low wall fence dividing our houses, bolting and locking the small gate behind him, to the sanctuary of our living room, where he argued the latest offerings of the newspapers with my father or just sat on one of our easy chairs, covered his face with an old newspaper, and dozed off. Since Uncle Happiness had not brought him any presents, he had no qualms about suggesting that my uncle was not presenting the whole picture.

'Some people sleep in the streets,' Adeyemo said, 'many die in winter. There are many poor people suffering.'

'There are some poor people,' Uncle Happiness conceded, 'but they are very few, usually people who don't want to work hard, and a poor man in America is a rich man in Nigeria. Everyone has a car except for a few people, very few. And nobody sleeps outside except maybe some mad people who escape from where they are kept. You know there are houses even for mad people. There are houses where you can just walk in and sleep, and in the morning you go and face your work.'

'There is unemployment, thousands of unemployed people. I saw the figures in the paper this afternoon.'

'Don't believe what those newspapers say; they are controlled by Jews and Russians who want to cause trouble in America. Unemployment in America? When they are begging you to come and work. Every shop you pass, everywhere they are looking for workers. You are very funny, sir. There is nothing like unemployment in America. Don't mind what those papers say; they are just making trouble.'

My mother kept out of the argument; she served Adeyemo a turkey drumstick and went to the dining table to look at her shop's accounts, while Uncle Happiness duelled with our neighbour, pitting the evidence of his naked eyes and the evidence of the naked eyes of close and trusted friends against what Adeyemo had read in trouble-making newspapers published by Jews and Russians.

For me there was no doubt at the time that Uncle Happiness was telling the truth and Adeyemo was just a loud-mouthed, interfering ignoramus who was jealous of our uncle who lived in America and had come to spoil our evening out of spite. I felt like kicking his dried-up bony legs with scales the shape of a spider's web, which poked out of his frayed khaki shorts like broomsticks and which kept shivering as he argued, in a voice that sounded like a knife being filed against rock.

'That man is a wicked man, you have to watch him carefully,' Uncle Happiness said to my mother, sounding rather subdued, after Adeyemo left.

I retold Uncle Happiness's stories when school resumed, and since I was already a habitual liar in my own right, I added spices of my own here and there. And one day when my mother wasn't looking, I stuffed my cowboy outfit into my school bag and showed it off to my classmates. I was riding on a wave of sudden popularity when Millard, a part Nigerian, part Gambian, part Irish, part God-knows-what-else classmate, who had returned late from the holidays, heard my stories and said I was lying. There is nothing more painful to a ten-year-old habitual liar than being called a liar, especially when he has told lies, and

8

I launched at Millard immediately we stepped out for break. It was not much of a fight, mainly pushing and shoving and threatening, but a teacher saw us and we spent the rest of the day standing under the sun in the football field.

I wrote to Uncle Happiness religiously, and once in a long while he replied and sent a present through someone who was visiting from America. We began to expect him every Christmas and then the Easter after. My mother, not wanting to be taken by surprise again, would have the curtains washed and buy new bedsheets for our guest room. On some rainy evenings our expectancy became so great that when someone knocked on the door we would exchange glances, and then I would walk nervously to open it, and before the door was open I'd hear my mother's voice behind me asking who it was, and it would be Adeyemo or one of my father's friends from the office not Uncle Happiness.

Once, when I was about thirteen, there was a great flurry around the house. Well-dressed young women came and went in large numbers; my mother wrote addresses, made phone calls, collected photographs. It turned out that she was searching for a wife for my Uncle Happiness. With time a candidate was chosen, and my mother began to wait for some papers from America to apply for a visa for the chosen one, impatiently tearing envelopes from our mailbox to shreds even though they had only Nigerian postmarks, but the papers did not come. And then Uncle Happiness was to come himself and have a look at his would-be bride. This time he gave a date, airline and flight number, and new curtains were quickly installed in our house and new bedsheets in the guest room, and the house was swept and scrubbed every day till all the hair on the plain blue living room carpet was almost gone, but Uncle Happiness did not come and did not give any reason for not coming. And that excitement finally died, like

9

an abnormal pregnancy that appears and disappears, begins to grow rapidly and then slowly and painfully miscarries.

◆

Eighteen years after his miraculous appearance in our house on a rainy Lagos evening, I sat benumbed in the living room of Uncle Happiness's two-bedroom apartment off Martin Luther King Jr. Avenue in Oakland, CA, a few blocks away from a BART rail line, reflecting that no matter how well you prepare yourself for disappointment, you are never prepared enough because a little shred of hope will continue to straggle along, ducking in the corners of your mind, and when disappointment comes it will seek out that straggling hope and crush it ruthlessly.

The brown sofa on which I sat was a massive semi-circle; it took up more than two-thirds of the living room, but each thread on it sagged as though someone had painstakingly pulled on every one of them. The sofa faced a huge cabinet that rose nearly to the ceiling. Someone had taken a sharp object and made marks all over the cabinet. Rusted cassette decks, amplifiers and turntables were piled on it in no particular order, like junk. In the centre was an ancient 26-inch TV which surprisingly showed bright pictures, but you couldn't hear what was being said because of a constant vicious hiss that came from the back of it. The walls of the living room, originally painted white, suffered from a spreading spotted grey eczema. On the floor was a carpet long trampled to a dusty-milk death; its farthest edges showed that, while alive, it had had green and yellow designs. A fierce smell, an oppressive compound of cigarette smoke and frying oil, sweat and damp, decay and despair ruled the room.

And there were these big, taciturn men, four of them. Each came in noiselessly, grunted greetings all round, gave me a quick second look and went into the kitchen, loaded a plate with rice and beans and chicken stew and came and sat on the sofa, facing the hissing TV. Then they fell on the rice and beans with a vengeance and never looked up till their plates were clean. I tried to be friendly as my uncle was not there. When I called from the airport, after the initial shrieks of excitement that I had finally arrived and how he had been looking forward to my coming and how everything would be taken care of soon, he said he had to go for a very, very important business appointment. He gave me the address, which I already had, told me to take a cab, that he would refund the fare later, and told me I'd find the key under the doormat if no one answered the bell, and then he hung up before I could ask any questions. So I ended up in that incredible decayed room of big, diseased furniture and big men who materialised without warning, and I said to the men: 'I'm Happiness's elder sister's son. I just came in from Nigeria this afternoon,' and managed to take their attention away from the hissing TV.

'Oh, welcome, hope it was a good trip, how are things at home?' etc. etc.

I know that for those who have gone away bad news of home is in a sense good news, for each time they hear of worsening economic desperation, armed robberies and assassinations and political crises they are reassured that they were right to leave, that whatever frustrations and humiliations they have to face in the strange land are well worth it. If home is such a terrible place, you may even manage to hold homesickness at bay a little. So I obliged them with the necessary horror stories. There was hardly any need to make up anything, for the country I had left the day before was a pretty rotten place. The second chapter of the protests against the military government which had annulled presidential elections held the year before was heating up; demonstrators had been killed in scores; petroleum workers were on strike again and there were long queues and fist-and-club-fights

11

at fuel stations; the police had not been paid for months and rumours said most of them had taken to armed robbery; cars were snatched at gunpoint every hour, houses raided every day sometimes at midday; one of the few boom areas in the economy was paid assassination; husbands woke up and walked away from their homes forever, leaving their wives to feed eight or nine ravenous mouths. My listeners shook their heads in amazement and duly exclaimed their horror; one was so grateful he went and bought a six-pack of Heineken for me from a store down the road.

And then it was time to sleep. Uncle Happiness was not yet back so one of them helped me put my suitcase and bag away into one of the bedrooms among tall stacks of bags, packing cases and dirty clothes. He pulled out a mattress for me from a pile of worn ones and set it in a corner of the room; he threw a sheet over it and gave me a worn comforter as it was getting cold, at least it was for me. And he knelt down on his own mattress which he set beside mine, prayed for about five minutes and then quickly filled the room with snores. And I lay awake listening to him all night.

I hadn't planned to stay with Uncle Happiness even though, on the two occasions I'd spoken to him from Nigeria, he had shouted his enthusiasm about my coming to America and had told me everything would be taken care of soon. I knew that a man who hadn't come home in eighteen years, who had set my mother searching the length and breadth of Nigeria for a wife and then lost his nerve when one was found couldn't be doing too well. My mother had a neat way of burying disturbing things deep inside her and for the last few years she had buried Uncle Happiness and smoothed his grave over. When I began discussing my American trip with her she hadn't mentioned her brother once.

I'd planned to stay with Kurubo, the Hook to his friends (a

12

tribute to his woman-chasing prowess), a friend through secondary school and university who'd left for America five years before. I'd spoken to the Hook a number of times by phone, calls that cut quite a hole in my pocket, and he had said he would gladly put me up until I found my feet. He had always sounded encouraging.

'Man, you'll be fine. A few problems at the beginning like in anything else, but you'll find you've made the best decision of your life, and, of course, I'll be there to ease things for you. You'll really be com-for-table. I just moved to a new place, three massive bedrooms, lotta room, lovely beds, excellent for balling. We are going to have a swell time. You need to see da black American chicks, you need to see them. You'll lose your mind. I guarantee you, your mind will burst. Just give me a call when you sort out the visa and flight arrangements and all that crap, and I'll lay on some welcoming pussy for you. Can't wait to see you, my man.'

That was my kind of talk, and though from previous experience I'd learnt to be extremely cautious about people's promises, I'd hoped that, even if I didn't get any welcoming pussy, I'd at least get a roof over my head and a bed to sleep in for a couple of months. And what happened? I finally got the visa and called the Hook's number: *I can't come to the phone right now but if you leave your name, number and a message after the beep blah blah blah.* So I left a message after the beep. I called again the next day at three o'clock in the afternoon so that it would be about six a.m. California time when the Hook wouldn't have gone out, and what did I get? *I can't come to the phone* and so on. So I left a message again, and I said to myself that maybe the Hook was out of town, and I said in the message that I'd call again in two days at about the same time, that is one day before my flight was to leave, and I called again, and of course it was *I can't come to the phone . . .* So I left yet another message, flight

13

number, time of arrival, all the details I could think of, and I said them twice, as clearly as possible, so that nothing would be missed. As I walked out of the business centre I began preparing for disappointment, but that little bit of hope continued to hide in the corner of my mind: the roomy new place, the beds excellent for balling, even the welcoming pussy.

And of course the bastard wasn't even at Oakland Airport. And I was tired and sick – I'd been flying for the last twenty hours: Lagos – London – New York – Oakland. Construction work was going on at Oakland Airport and the indifferent streams of brisk passengers of all colours surging through narrow lanes marked by yellow tape and demarcation boards with crude arrows, bumping into cement-covered workmen while struggling to control their trolleys and children, the general air of chaos and desperation in the airport, aggravated my disorientation, and above all else, I wanted to sit on my suitcase and weep.

I had, being a prudent man, called Uncle Happiness twice from Nigeria as insurance after I started hearing *I can't come to the phone* . . . from the Hook's answering machine. However, Uncle Happiness was to be the very last resort. I had the number of a family friend from Nigeria, Ego, who had married well – to a wealthy Nigerian doctor – and I'd been told they lived somewhere nearby. My mother had told her mother I was leaving for America and her mother had promised to call and tell her and her doctor husband. Ego's family had been transformed by her marriage; her father now had a Mercedes Benz 230 from Belgium, ten years old but well painted. Before his son-in-law in America gave him the Mercedes, he had only a smoking, wrecked Toyota Crown from the early seventies, which could no longer climb the slightest incline, so that if he wanted to go anywhere he would first have to rack his old head to determine if there was

14

a flyover or slope on the road between where he was and where he wanted to get to, and if there was he would take his walking stick and walk to the nearest bus stop, grumbling all the way about what had happened to the country.

Our families had been friends for as far back as I could remember, but I'd never had time for Ego; she was so well behaved, so proper it was nauseating. She stooped very low to greet older people, her eyes respectfully averted, rushed to pick up any baby in the room and to make all the appropriate noises about how nice it looked, or how well it was growing, and kissed and fondled it; she was always dressed properly, frocks and skirt suits in the right colours, her hair set in the same proper perm she's worn all her adult life. She was what people call marriage material, not even one little scandal I can remember, only one or two boyfriends before the wealthy doctor came and carried her off, boyfriends who were all as well behaved as she was, who bowed and scraped before her parents and also fondled and kissed babies, insipid assholes. So I wasn't full of enthusiasm about calling Ego, but my only other option was Uncle Happiness so I called Ego.

'Who are you staying with?' was the first thing she wanted to know.

'Well, I've sort of just – em – just got in, sort of, and I'm going to be staying with Kurubo, maybe you know him, tall, slim guy. We were at school together, but he is out of town and I need—'

'Obi, I'm sorry, our place is too far away, and I didn't mention to my husband that you were coming. But when you settle down properly, give us a call. I have to see someone and I'm already late. Nice talking to you. Take care.'

Bitch! Back in Lagos she would have been grateful if I had asked any favour of her, but as I was to learn again and again, America turns your world upside down. That's how I came to be stuck with Uncle Happiness and the house that smelt of stale sweat and hopelessness.

◆

I moved out after three days by which time I was close to committing suicide. I'd called the Hook's number ten times in two days and I'd heard (you guessed it) *I can't come to the phone right now* – and I'd left abject message after abject message. I'd begun to wonder if coming to Oakland had been such a good idea: I had cousins on my father's side in Houston – we hadn't heard much from them in years, but it was unlikely they'd be worse off than Uncle Happiness. I'd chosen Oakland because everyone I'd spoken to, and the Hook in particular, said California was wonderful for a new immigrant even with Governor Pete Wilson and the imminence of Proposition 187. It had excellent weather and a huge economy that offered many opportunities. I was looking through the window of Uncle Happiness's living room at the empty street below, tossing Oakland and Houston and the mocking announcement on the Hook's answering machine about in my mind, when I remembered that Andrew lived in Oakland too, and I had his number.

Andrew had been on the same floor with me in my final year in university, a few doors away from my room. He was a short, nervous, nerdy, apologetic fellow with a square face and a bad right leg, which he broke the first day he tried, as a kid, to play football and which he dragged along painfully as he walked. He was doing medicine, but even for a medical student he was terribly studious. Some days he went to the classrooms at the crack of dawn and studied till after midnight, taking only one break to eat a snack in a nearby shop. He was a born-again Christian who had the misfortune to live in the same row of rooms as the most committed sinners in the university.

16

Two rooms away from him was Ilya who liked to boast that he'd killed a man in a fight and got all his sex from rape. The only time he was ever reported, he spent only two days in a police station and then returned to the university in triumph, surrounded by a singing, cheering band of hangers-on, members of the secret fraternity he led. The girl he raped quickly transferred to another university and after that his victims kept their humiliation to themselves. The Hook, one of the randiest men ever created, lived at the end of the corridor. I shared a room with Bronzo, another sex-crazed monster, who screamed piercingly when he came, the wild death-welcoming cry of a prisoner being released from his pain. (I realise now with hindsight that Bronzo's screams while coming probably had less to do with sexual pleasure than with the need to advertise to all of us that he was having good sex. For among our bunch of teenage undergrads, the awe and envy of your friends was a lot more important than the most thundering orgasm.) Commando ran a gambling den in the room next to Andrew's; the card games often ended in fights when someone just back from a visit home lost his entire pocket money in the blink of an eye and refused to accept defeat gracefully. It was among these and other evil people that Andrew was condemned to spend his final year in medicine.

Bronzo would stop him in the corridor after a long night of studying and shake his penis at Andrew and bleat, 'Andy boy, can you lend me one of your succulent sisters in Christ just for a night; you know I'm not greedy, just for one night. I guarantee top quality of service.' Andrew would smile nervously and say, 'Bronzo, as soon as you accept Jesus Christ as your personal saviour, you'll find that the things of the flesh are not as important as you think,' and he would walk past to his room while Bronzo continued bleating behind him, 'Just for one night, Andy my boy. Let me teach her a thing or two. And you too, you can watch. I'll give you full video rights. Your life will never be the same afterwards.'

Andrew took all the insults and provocations like a saint. He hoped perhaps to convert us with the example of his grace and was always willing to share the word of God. When anyone was broke he would listen politely to Andrew, knowing that if you seemed close enough to conversion, he would buy you a meal or two, or invite you to a retreat or other church get-together where the food was always abundant and given freely.

Midway through our final year he seemed to score a big coup – the Hook suddenly became a born-again Christian. Every Sunday, for several weeks, the Hook would turn out in a dark blazer, white shirt, pretty tie, khaki trousers and black leather shoes and go with Andrew to church, a little Bible tucked under his arm. We made fun of his new piety for a while and then gave up, astounded by the change that had come over him, and also a little worried: if this could happen to the Hook it could probably happen to any of us. Then a scandal broke – the Hook had made one of the sisters in Christ, Franca, pregnant. Franca was gorgeous: a smooth face as fresh as a mint currency note and the kind of body you see in a swimsuit and you nearly go bonkers. Every time she walked past a group of guys someone would cry: oh, how could such a lovely creature follow those born-again crazies? Franca left the university and never returned; the Hook, mission accomplished, went back to being one of the boys. Andrew forgave him even that and continued trying to take him back to the narrow path.

Inside my wallet I found Andrew's number on the back of a crumpled business card. I had scribbled it there out of politeness, the day one of his sisters in Christ from university saw me on Broad Street, about two weeks before I left Lagos, and told me he was now in Oakland and made me promise to give him a call to tell him they were all fine and praying for him. I'd wondered

18

at the time how a man like Andrew got to America: he'd seemed the sort that would be content with any job as a doctor in any part of Nigeria for the near-starvation wages doctors are paid. And then I'd forgotten about Andrew – he wasn't the type of person I planned to have anything to do with in the States. But after three days in Uncle Happiness's house I would have considered becoming a born-again Christian to get away from that place. Andrew was out the first two times I called, but he answered the third time, and when I told him I was in Oakland and needed a place to stay, he started shouting praises to the Lord into the phone in his nervous way.

'Of course you can stay with me until you get your own place. I have only a studio apartment, but we can manage. Just tell me where you are, and I'll come and pick you up.'

I gave him the address and he said he would be there in about thirty minutes, that he lived at another end of Oakland but he would come by the freeway and would probably get there in less, but to be on the safe side he would say thirty minutes. As soon as I dropped the phone I went to the room where my things were and began to pack. I wrote a note for Uncle Happiness saying I'd run into a good friend from Lagos outside on the street and had gone over to stay with him for a while.

◆

Uncle Happiness had finally appeared at noon the day after my arrival. He had swept into the house in a massive black coat and a bright red beret, hollering for me: 'Oh my dear sister's son! My own Obi!'; he was looking as round as ever. His stomach had grown even bigger, but his head seemed to have shrunk, creating a comical disproportion between head and body. He still rolled forward on boomerang legs, still bellowed out his words even when you were right there in front of him, but the nearly permanent lines of happiness on his face were gone, and when he laughed now it was as if he was merely pretending to laugh. He seemed shocked when he saw me, as though he'd entered the house expecting to see a boy of ten, the same one who went around Lagos with him in matching cowboy clothes, and saw instead a man of twenty-eight, a head taller than him, who watched him warily with the eyes of a snake. He went through the motions of hugging me, of bellowing how big I'd grown, even taller than your uncle, but he sounded unsure of himself as if I might be an impostor who had stolen the identity of his sister's son. As he fumbled through his apologies for not being able to pick me up at the airport and for being away from home for so long, he shot nervous glances at me and stared for long moments at the filthy rug and at his shoes. He said he'd been involved in very, very important business and he, in fact, had just gotten away because of me, to see how I was managing. I wondered what sort of business kept one away from one's home all night.

Uncle Happiness hurried off again only minutes after, telling me he still had very important business to attend to but promising to tear himself away as soon as possible. On my second evening alone with the four huge men, I tried to find out who they were and what jobs they did. They all had short English names, Sam, Ken, Bob, etc. that sounded false, names manufactured for use in America, and they all pretended not to have heard my questions about what they did. I was soon to learn that to ask my countrymen and women in America questions about their jobs was most indiscreet; the successful ones and the liars told you before you asked, others maintained a stony silence or made vague sounds, and many people have acquired lifelong enemies just by asking too insistently.

Uncle Happiness returned at about eleven, smiling like he'd won the lottery and smelling heavily of alcohol. He began hollering my name from the staircase of the two-storied building with six apartments, and I wondered momentarily how his neighbours coped with him. When he got back, I was alone in the living room of big, diseased furniture, trying to read a novel; the others had gone to bed. He clasped my right hand in his in a tight grip, smiling and looking into my eyes all the while. I smiled back.

'My sister's son, my darling sister's son, Obi the Giant, I'm so happy to see you. You don't know how happy I've been since you came. You can ask the people I was with at the business meeting until a few minutes ago, I couldn't keep my mind on what we were discussing. So they told me, they said, "Happiness, you are no longer paying attention to what we are discussing here; you can go and see your sister's son and leave us alone to continue our meeting." And I thanked them and left. Let's go out and have a drink. I'm sure you drink beer now. What is your brand? Becks? Heineken? Guinness?'

I didn't think he was in any condition to take in more beer and I politely refused. He frowned suddenly, and I knew I had offended him.

'Uncle,' I said, 'I'm very tired, but tomorrow we can go out any time you like.'

I hoped he wouldn't be in even worse shape the next day.

'Let's go,' he said, pulling my arm impatiently. 'I left my important meeting to come and take you out, and you say you won't go?'

The way he said it, with an angry undercurrent in his voice and a desperate look on his face, as though if I continued to decline he would throw me out on the street the next moment, left me no choice. I followed him downstairs, my apprehension increasing as he engaged himself in a violent, muttering argument on the way. His car was a wide antique Olds with as many dents and scratches as a Lagos taxi cab; the seat was so mushy it felt like sitting in a swamp.

Uncle Happiness swung the car into the road with a grunt, and we shot down the street trailed by the loud, hoarse groaning of the exhaust. We hit the junction with Martin Luther King Jr. Street at top speed and after a quick glance to his left, Uncle Happiness threw the car into the traffic, missing another wide old car that was cruising in the inner lane by inches.

'Useless people,' Uncle Happiness said, 'people in this useless country don't know how to drive. Why is he playing on the road as if it's his father's private property?'

He swung from lane to lane, overtaking, cutting in, flying past yellow lights and at least one red one, cursing every other driver on the road for driving like cows, pregnant women, idiots, drunkards; the ubiquitous liquor store neon signs offering Budweiser, Coors and whatnot madly racing past us. My heart pounded; I gripped my seat, and then the door handle. Now and again I muttered: 'Take it easy, Uncle,' but he ignored me. I wondered which of many catastrophes would befall us that night. Would he knock someone down or smash into another car? Would we be stopped by the police and he imprisoned for driving under the influence? Would he hit a truck and kill us both? But by a miracle we reached the freeway safely, and though Uncle Happiness stepped on the gas pedal with all his strength, and the groaning of the exhaust began to sound like the rumble of an earthquake, the car was unable to reach an unsafe speed. I relaxed a bit.

Freed from cursing other drivers and jumping across lanes, Uncle Happiness began to let off a torrent of words:

'I'm so happy you are here, I'm so happy. You don't know how happy I am. When you phoned me to say you were coming, I was overjoyed. That's always what I wanted. You can ask your mother, I wrote to her many years ago to tell her that once you finished your first degree, you should come over here. You know, this is the greatest country in the world, there's no place like

America. With your intelligence, the money you'll make here in one month when you've fully settled down is more than you'll make in Nigeria in ten years. You know I negotiated for a big house for us, a four-bedroom house where you'd be comfortable, but they ate my money. This country is full of criminals as you will soon find out. I paid them for the house and for the furniture all at the same time, a new fridge, TV, seats, everything new; I wanted you to be very comfortable, but they took my money and disappeared. So please manage this our house for a while. I know it's not very comfortable, but please manage the house for now. I am making many arrangements, and everything will be all right soon. Those people staying with me, I just do it to help people who have come newly and don't know where to stay. It is a way of helping them out for a while until they can find their own houses and settle down. I had planned to get the new house, and then we would move there, and I would keep this one just for helping people, but they ate my money like I told you so we will manage this one for a short time, then I will finish the arrangements I'm making. Then everything will be all right. I don't want you to suffer even for a minute in this country while I'm alive. Please just manage that house for a short time. I am making plans to take care of everything, and I am sure things will work out the way I have planned. You know, you and I together we'll do a lot of things, you are very educated, that's all I need. My greatest problem in this country is that I did not go to school for very long. That's why things have sometimes been difficult for me. But I have tried my best. God is my witness. He knows I am not a lazy man, that I have never taken any man's money. I have tried my best, but without education you will have problems in this country. But since you are very educated and very intelligent, I will bring my experience, to be in this country for twenty-four years is not a joke, you will bring your brain, and together we will get whatever we want. Those who

23

have looked down on Happiness will soon know that I have people in this world, educated people.'

And thus he went on, urgent and out of control like gas rushing out of a burst high-pressure pipe. My sides hurt from the cold night air which poured in from the wound down window on his side; I bore the discomfort silently as it was unthinkable that I would interrupt his charged monologue for a matter as frivolous as winding up the window on his side.

'You and I will do so much together. Let us just manage the house for a while, and then when you settle down, we can move to any place we want. Your mother, my sister, she does not understand. But you are a man, you will understand. I wanted a wife, yes, I wanted a wife. But you do not bring a woman all the way from home to come here and suffer. I was doing well and I had money, but there were many things I was working on at that time, and people cheated me and took my money. I have suffered in America because I did not go to school for long. They took all my money at that time, and I had to start from the beginning, but your mother will not understand. She will say get married, get married, how can you get married when you make plans and then evil people come and take your money from you, and you have to start from the beginning again. The money I have made in this country is so much you will not believe how much money I have made. I am not a lazy man, I work very hard, and I have made a lot of money, but thieves have stolen all of it. I tried to tell your mother but she will not listen to me. I know you understand better than she does, you know women are not understanding. Once they have made up their minds, you will not be able to change it for them. But you are now a man, I know you will understand. Let us just manage things for a short while.'

We drove through a night prettily sprinkled with light. Tail-lights and headlights and clusters of streetlights glinted off the brilliant dividers on the road, mighty hotels bursting with brilliance suddenly appeared on the tops of hills, as though by an illusionist's trick. And the lights of a town at the bottom of a valley would hang in the air for seconds, an endless blanket of distant fireflies, and then vanish, only to re-appear at the other side of a hill. Even now when I can easily tell which distant neon light belongs to a Denny's restaurant and which one advertises a shopping mall, my freeway nights are sometimes almost as magical as that first experience.

Uncle Happiness talked and talked. He spoke more to himself than to me, simultaneously making excuses for his failures and convincing himself that I was a new fountain of hope, and finally he managed to control the disquiet in him that he had tried to defeat with alcohol and failed, the disquiet he had vented at other vehicles in traffic and at his ancient Oldsmobile. Towards the end of the drive, as he exited from the freeway and headed home, the drink he had said we were going to have entirely forgotten, he was in a calmer mood. With growing conviction, he repeated his story about the furnished four-bedroom house he'd tried to get, and how he'd been cheated and about all the money he'd made and lost, and his hope that he and I working together (he contributing his twenty-four-year experience of America and I my intelligence and education) would make enormous amounts of money and live in luxury happily ever after. I listened to all this in silence, marvelling at this fifty-year-old child who hid away from the world that had beaten him in fantasy houses of his own construction, the way, as a child, I had escaped from the tedium of life around me by converting myself into Captain Darkie, a character in one of my boys' comics, the leader of an invincible band of British commandos decimating the slit-eyed Japanese in the jungles of Burma during the Second World War.

When we got back to the house that smelt of stale sweat and

failure, he pleaded with me once more to manage the house for a little while, that everything would soon be all right. Needless to say, I didn't share his optimism. I felt trapped in his decayed house and repelled by the dreams in which he tried to hide. I'd come to America to seek success not to keep company with failure.

◆

I phoned Uncle Happiness after I'd spent a day at Andrew's to appease any ill feelings he might have had towards me for leaving his house the way I did. I'd given him five hundred dollars the day before I left to get me a social security card from a friend of his who he said provided documents for illegals, and I was afraid that if he felt offended at my leaving I might never get the card or get my money back.

'I hope your friend's place is fine,' Uncle Happiness said over the phone. 'Please manage with your friend for a while; everything is going to be all right soon, and we can move to another house, just you and me.'

Instead of feeling hurt, Uncle Happiness sounded rather happy that I had left. The elements of his fantasies were apparently quite easy to re-arrange; perhaps if I'd told him I now lived in the street, he might have cheerfully said, please manage the pavements for a while, everything will soon be all right, and so on.

He called me at Andrew's about two weeks later to say that he would get my social security card later that day, and I could collect it from him at five p.m. At the time the streets were still unfamiliar to me so I left Andrew's place a good hour before five and got to Uncle Happiness's early. His Olds was parked outside. I went up to his apartment and rang the bell. He let me in with the habitual loud exclamations and expressions of joy at seeing me and introduced me to a man with the smooth fleshy face of an overweight child, who could easily have been a very light-skinned black man or a Latino, or a bit of each. In a cream jacket, beige shirt, red bow-tie and black trousers, he looked like he was on his way to a dinner. His round glasses gave him an academic air. He was smoking a foul-smelling pipe which had aroused all the other smells imprisoned in the living room. Uncle Happiness introduced him as Mr Cassidy – who helped people.

'I help people *all right*; you can say I'm a *philanthropist*,' Mr Cassidy said with great emphasis, and he then burst out laughing for no apparent reason. Uncle Happiness joined in and I joined them, too, since everyone else was laughing so hard. From Mr Cassidy's accent I deduced he was a Nigerian trying to imitate the roller-skate rhythm of African-American English with very little success.

'Are you the guy who needs the social security card?'

I nodded.

'I already gave it to Happiness. Happiness is a *good* man, a very good man, and a darn good *customer*,' and Mr Cassidy burst out laughing again. This time I let him and Uncle Happiness do the laughing.

Uncle Happiness took the card out of his pocket and handed it to me. I looked at it with excitement and fear. Armed with this little piece of paper, I would be able to work, to begin to pursue my own modest American dream (save some money, do a good MBA and then a nice job in a good corporation), but at the same time I wondered for how long I'd be able to carry around a forged document without being detected in this land of mega-computers. All it would take would be for one of them to pick up a tiny questionable aspect of the card and then – prison or deportation, both probably.

'That's the *real* thing,' Mr Cassidy said, reading my mind. 'It came from Uncle Sam *himself*, and you can ask Happiness. I've been getting papers for Happiness for *years* and none of his people has ever had a problem. Right, Happiness?'

'That's true,' my uncle said.

There's of course always a first time, I thought, and with my kind of luck that first time could be me. But, anyway, what was to be done? I couldn't possibly to go the Immigration and Naturalization Service and say: 'Hey guys, I came into your country on a visitor's visa, but I really would like to stay, get a job, save some money, go to graduate school and get a nice corporate job. Can you let me have a green card to help me along?' This peril-strewn path of forged papers and shady men was the only one open to me.

Suddenly inspired by that alert distrust of everything and everybody which Lagos teaches you very quickly, I turned to Mr Cassidy and asked in an innocent-sounding voice:

'How much does it cost to get this card?'

'Three hundred bucks,' he said. 'Didn't Happiness tell you yet?'

I didn't answer but looked at my uncle who had taken five hundred dollars from me for the card. He turned away and fastened his eyes on one of the eczematous walls of his living room. He shrank even further in my eyes, became a bald-headed wrinkled worm; not just a failure who filled his head with childish fantasies but also a small time crook who would steal from his own blood.

Christ, Gandhi and a Girl with Brown Hair

Andrew looked exactly the way he'd looked at university: the same nerdy, apologetic, dark brown, square-faced ugliness, the same thick glasses with cheap black frames, the same painful limp, even the same anonymous short-sleeved shirt, the stripes of which were so faded you could hardly tell that it had ever been striped. He smiled nervously when I let him into Uncle Happiness's living room and hesitantly called me Oh-Bye – the hip version of my name used by friends and classmates in university – as though he was afraid I'd get angry with him for taking liberties. He held out his two hands limply in front of him. I was unsure whether he intended to take my hand in both his, give me a hug, or help me carry my things which were lying behind me just inside the door. I shook his right hand warmly; it was the least I could do for someone who had so enthusiastically offered to house me. As I left Uncle Happiness's house, I shook the dust off my feet.

I'd seen very little of Oakland since I arrived, and the streets Andrew and I drove through were depressing: they struck me as places from which hope and ambition had been wrung out. People neglected or couldn't afford to put a fresh coat of paint on their homes, dead and dying cars littered the sides of the streets, some of which were so empty it seemed as though everyone had been wiped out by a plague. Andrew took a long route to show me the really bad parts in West Oakland, the way a Londoner might show off the West End. At first I didn't see much difference between what he said were the really bad drug-devastated parts and the not-so-bad areas we'd passed through earlier. Then I noticed the way the insides of some houses had been eaten up as though by a billion famished ants, leaving only outer walls, frames and roofs, the boarded-up auto repair shops covered by generations of graffiti, the empty lots on which moss was spreading, and the people, ragged and stranded, standing on pavements, sitting outside shops, staring into space.

'At night this can be a very dangerous area,' Andrew said with visible revulsion, 'that is when the drug dealers begin business, and then you have the shootings and the police sirens. I think they are all asleep during the day.'

The African immigrant sometimes exhibits as much bitterness

29

towards his African-American cousins as the worst white racist. Confronted with scenes like those we saw during that drive through West Oakland and the terrible images of inner-city violence and despair on TV, the success-obsessed immigrant wants to get as far away as possible, psychically if not physically, from that horrible pit. He violently rejects any identification with what strikes him as irreversible disaster, the way one might disown and denounce a family member suffering from incurable alcoholism and kleptomania. It was that sort of rejection I saw on Andrew's face, and that was perhaps why he took me on that tour of West Oakland – to teach me early on how to be revolted by the inner city and the African-Americans who, no matter how successful some of them may become, are in our minds chained to the inner city.

Andrew's own place was on the second of five floors in an apartment block on Lee Street, off Grand Avenue. It was nicer than the other parts of the city we'd passed through. It was a hilly area with apartment blocks of many shapes and sizes on which the paint was generally not too weathered. Perhaps because it was so hilly there, some of the buildings looked from a distance as though they were supporting each other. Lee Street was a few blocks away from Lake Merritt, vast and radiant in the afternoon sun; standing outside the place where Andrew lived, you could see the tops of the tall office buildings of downtown Oakland.

His room was large and airy, but the crowd of religious posters on the wall and the room's regimented tidiness made me a little claustrophobic. I took a seat by the wide window that looked out on to two rows of parked cars. Andrew handed me a glass of orange juice (the other option was Diet Pepsi), and he put my things away in the wardrobe with the cheerful efficiency of a professional servant. He offered to quickly warm a meal for me, but I declined: I was getting uncomfortable with Andrew's excessive kindness. After the mandatory comments about how sick Nigeria currently was and the usual cries of horror, we began talking about our university days. Andrew had heard from someone that the Hook lived near Oakland, but had not met up with him; he had surprisingly pleasant memories of the Hook.

'He was a very nice person. I think he wanted to be a born-again Christian, but he was confused and found it difficult to make up his mind. It was partly immaturity, I think. He couldn't have been more than twenty in his final year.'

I didn't say anything to that. As I remembered it the Hook, young though he was, had no difficulty in making up his mind that what he wanted was the incredibly desirable Franca, not the grace of the Lord Jesus Christ. Andrew remembered me as his good friend; he said I encouraged him a great deal when he was preparing for his final year exams. I had no such memory, but nodded in agreement.

'You always stood by your friends,' Andrew said, implying that he was one of such friends, and I nodded again. Not being as depraved as Bronzo, the Hook and the others, I hadn't directly tormented Andrew, but I remembered with shame how loudly I had laughed at the lewd jokes made at his expense. His own recollections were entirely different, and I was amazed at how his mind had completely revised the past like a Stalinist historian, retroactively awarding himself the friendship of people who had never hidden from him their contempt for and derision of him, transforming cynical bastards into nice young men and loyal friends with clean hearts, only a little confused and slightly distracted by matters of the flesh.

Though it was a Saturday, Andrew soon had to leave for work after I had reassured him that I was comfortable and didn't need anything other than to make a few phone calls and get some sleep. He told me later that he had two jobs – one at a kidney dialysis plant in a small town outside Oakland and another job he didn't name in addition to receiving training at a school for Africa-bound missionaries. All three kept him occupied sixteen hours a day Monday to Friday and ten hours on Saturdays.

I'd mentioned to him that I had to make calls to Nigeria and that I would pay for my calls when the bill came, but Andrew would not hear of my paying; after much wrangling we agreed that we'd split the bill in two. The day the phone bill came, about a month later, I was sitting on the chair by the window, which had become my favourite spot in the room, looking out at the street. Andrew was opening his mail when a gasp of horror escaped from his throat. I thought he'd received bad news from home. The bill hung from the suddenly lifeless fingers of his right hand. I took it from him and saw that it was for more than two hundred dollars. Apart from two local numbers, I'd made all the calls (seven long ones to Nigeria). Though I didn't quite gasp like Andrew, the bill hit me very hard. I said I'd pay for every call I'd made and this time he didn't argue.

I called Lagos as soon as Andrew had left for one of his two jobs. Robo, my girlfriend, sounded sleepy on the phone, then she recognised my voice and gave a heart-warming yell of delight.

As I write this, I'm struck by how different my experience of leaving Nigeria would have been if the telephone hadn't been invented. The telephone simultaneously reduces the distance between the exile and the homeland and increases the pain of separation. A letter that would take weeks to arrive at its destination emphatically reminds the exile of distance, encourages coming to terms with separation, whereas the realization that what has been left behind is only a phonecall away prolongs the embrace of the past. Because of the miracle of the telephone, it is easy to go on believing that what you have been separated from hasn't been left behind at all, as a result of which the process of separation becomes confusing and messy, vulnerable to self-deception and the notorious frailties of the human heart.

'I was getting worried,' Robo said. 'I know we agreed you'd call first but when I hadn't heard from you I called the Hook's number yesterday morning and got the answering machine. I called again three hours later and still got the machine, and I really began to get worried. Of course I was just being silly – you guys could have gone out somewhere.'

I told her about the Hook not turning up at the airport and about the three days I spent in Uncle Happiness's house, omitting the grimmer details, but it was impossible to leave out of my voice the weight of accumulated disappointments.

'I'm so sorry,' Robo said, 'I can't believe the Hook could be so rotten to make all those promises and not even show up at the airport. Even if he had to travel he should have had someone to pick you up.'

'So, how are you?' I asked, anxious to move on to other things.

'What do you think? Miserable and missing you wretchedly already. America seems so far away, like another planet. My mum has been trying to cheer me up. Even my father's noticed something's wrong. "How's your friend?" he asked me the other day and I knew he meant you, of course, since you are the only one he calls "my friend". I imagine that calling your name would be too intimate for him so it's a kind of code between us, but this time I pretended I didn't have any idea who he was referring to. So he tried harder, "Your friend, you know, um . . . um . . . the boy, your friend," and I asked him again, "Daddy, which boy?" And he finally had to mention the unmentionable. "I mean Obi, isn't that the boy's name?" I told him you'd gone to America and he looked at me strangely as if checking to see if I was lying, then he changed the subject.'

Though Robo and I had been together, with a few breaks, some short, some long, for thirteen years, her father had still not become adjusted to the idea of *his* precious, only daughter sleeping with a young man with an arrogant walk and defiant eyes, who sometimes even sat on *his* settee in *his* cosy living room and was served *his* brandy and ate *his* food and looked through *his* books and *his* collection of old jazz albums. He was a tall man with a wrinkled, bitter face; I thought it was me at first, but Robo assured me that even when receiving cheques from the clients of his accountancy firm the look on his face was one of implacable hatred. I suspect his bitter face was responsible for turning Robo's mother, a pleasant enough woman, into a gloomy, nervous mound of incompetence. He had the opposite effect on Robo; it was her long and meandering laugh, like a pleasant cruise in lovely weather, and her wide-eyed smile of a naughty child that I fell for very badly. And also her smooth copper-burnished chocolate skin, with her slender face of understated beauty which you needed discernment to appreciate, and two small breasts, always in a state of agitation – Robo claimed they were too small for her to wear a bra so her nipples pushed out against her clothes, looking perennially erect. Even as I write this, that memory provokes a stirring in my underpants.

'So, how is Lagos?'

'More or less the way you left it. My father and I went to a meeting with clients in Ikoyi yesterday, and on our way out we got stuck on Awolowo Road because fuel queues had blocked the road in front of us and behind. We waited for two hours, and then we had to leave the driver there and walk all the way to Falomo where we took a taxi home. As usual, the place is full of rumours – you hear today the oil workers' strike is going to be called off, that a deal has been made, then you hear it hasn't. Please let's forget about this country for now and talk of better things. So, what are your first impressions of America?'

'I feel I haven't arrived here yet; I'm still probing at the edges. However, I've seen the inner city with my own eyes, and though I didn't see any actual violence, there was a sense in which I felt

I was watching people die slowly before my eyes. The area of Oakland where Andrew lives isn't bad at all, thank God. Have you seen my folks since I left?'

'Not yet. You know, I slept in your house the night you left. Your mum broke down as soon as you went into the immigration area and we couldn't follow any more. It was bad, Obi. Waxy and I tried to calm her down, but she just kept crying. She tried to stop but couldn't, and after a while we both joined in with her. She pleaded with me to stay when we got to your place and anyway I was in no condition to drive all the way home so we went to a business centre and I called my house. I slept in your room and the next morning it was like we were all still in mourning! It was really ridiculous. Your mum says she's going to get a phone for her shop even if she has to see the Head of State for it. Knowing her, you can be sure she'll have one in a month or two; she says she has to hear your voice at least once every fortnight, no matter what the cost is. And speaking of cost, if I don't stop all my *gisting*, this phone call will cost you a fortune.'

'No, it's not that expensive to call from America,' I lied quickly, anxious to keep the conversation going.

'Well, if you say so. I'll go to your place as soon as I can, check how your mum is doing. She really looked bad that day. I didn't know she could ever cry over anything so much though I've always known she loved you terribly.'

My mother had hovered around me while I checked in for the flight, guarded my passport and boarding pass jealously, eyeing the loafers who hung around the terminal building. She carefully examined the locks on my suitcase and the bag I was carrying on to the plane, interrogated me closely to make sure I'd not left anything behind, reminded me to take my Sunday-to-Sunday medicine in America regularly for the first few months – you know they don't know how to treat malaria there – and warned

35

me again and again about the evils that abounded in America: AIDS, random robbery and murder, etc. etc. If she could have, she'd have gone to the plane and opened it up to confirm that its engines were good enough to take her son safely to London, the first leg of my journey. And she would have demanded to see the pilot's licence. Crying is as alien to my mother as rain is to the Sahara desert; she sniffed and rubbed her eyes with a dry handkerchief at funerals until they became a bit red so that people wouldn't think her hard-hearted. The thought of her crying all night at my departure was heartbreaking.

Waxy was the nickname for my younger sister, Nwaka. I never called her that, for it represented in my mind her astonishing grownupness which had begun to frighten me in the last few years, and most acutely since she'd gone to the University of Lagos to study medicine. From the age of fifteen, her body had begun to explode dangerously in all directions, drawing battalions of lecherous admirers who haunted our house and, at least in my troubled mind, filled her room every evening at the hostel of the College of Medicine. She always carried herself with such maturity and grace that it seemed silly to worry about her, but in a city with armies of predators, ranging from student secret fraternity louts to sixty-year-old playboys who bought first class return tickets to Europe for their girlfriends as though they were buying bottles of Coke, a girl with a body like that was always in mortal danger. Nwaka was, like our mother, not a crying person. But we'd all been together in Lagos all our lives, in the same house or, since my elder sister, Adaku, got married, within a few miles of each other, and to them my going to America to live must have seemed like stepping into a void in the centre of the earth.

'I feel so alone,' Robo said in a voice that had suddenly gone from lively chattiness to quiet agony. 'Why did you have to go? *Why couldn't you have just stayed with me?*'

I felt like a farmer whose entire herd of cattle has gone berserk and bolted away into a surrounding forest. We'd gone over this for months and agreed that my going to America was the best thing for us (or I thought we'd agreed). She would visit after one year, when I had settled down a little, and then we'd jointly make plans for the future. The progress I thought we'd made in so many hours of painful, repetitive discussion had been erased by that agonised tone, the labour of many months had turned to dust in seconds.

I began to recite the arguments: Nigeria was certain to continue along a path of steady decline, blundering from one ridiculous crisis to another, and could at any time explode into ethnic or religious warfare or some combination of both. We needed to sink our roots as a family, in a stable, functioning, dynamic place; we needed to make a fresh start in 'a land of opportunity'. There was nothing for me in Nigeria, and the longer I remained there, the unhappier I would become, and it would, with time, begin to take a toll on our relationship. As it was now we would be apart for a while, but we would bear it knowing it was unavoidable; we would always keep in touch, always support each other.

'I know,' Robo said, her voice still soaked in pain, 'I'm just being stupid and soppy. Forgive me, I should try and reduce the things you have to bother about not increase them. I'm so sorry. It's just that I feel so alone. I can't remember the last time I couldn't see you every day.'

'It's going to be all right, darling,' I said, desperately believing myself. 'We're going to be fine.'

Burgess (the novelist, not the spy) wrote: 'Love [is] only a durable fire if the man [is] there to fill the coal-scuttle.' I strove to fill my own coal-scuttle from thousands of miles away. In long phone conversations with Robo about old friends, new crises and scandals, I pledged my love as often as I could, endlessly explaining why I had had to move to America, like a desperate salesman. In the process I savagely robbed my lean pockets to add to AT & T's overflowing cash vaults, but all my efforts ended in dismal failure.

◆

I was so tired, not having slept properly in five days, that I passed out immediately after the call, sprawled thoughtlessly across the bed. I was gently woken up by Andrew, who had slept on a spare mattress on the floor. He apologised profusely for rousing me, saying he only did so because I'd been sleeping since about noon the day before and he thought I might like to get up and have breakfast and maybe go to church. I was ravenously hungry and agreed to breakfast and, to show my gratitude to Andrew for taking me in, to church.

The church was in a small town about twenty-five miles from Oakland. On the way we passed beautiful rolling hills and valleys covered alternately by golden brown carpets of grass and luxuriant forests of cypress and eucalyptus. Small picturesque cottages huddled on hilltops, and office buildings nestled in seductively leafy landscapes, so perfectly realised you thought they were architect's models, not real functional structures. In minutes we went from urban exhaustion to idyllic parkland. Cars, jeeps, pick-ups and huge trucks sped past us on Highway 24. Andrew kept his old Volvo in the slow lane, gripping the steering wheel as though he were afraid someone would snatch it away from him.

The church was a simple, circular, cream-coloured building, topped by an elaborate roof of weathered, reddish-brown tiles which rose steeply from all sides and ended in a tall, narrow crest, pointing towards heaven. We were the only black people in the church. Andrew led the way to two seats at the back even though there were rows of vacant seats in front, which made me think of the infamously segregated buses of the old deep South. Our fellow worshippers were laundered, starched and ironed to a spotless, unwrinkled cleanliness and familiness – father, mother, child or two, sometimes a grandmother, seated together in visible righteousness. These, I thought, looked like people incapable of even *thinking* of sin or the merest indiscretion. The light seats of stainless steel and black leather, like in an office reception room, took away some of the church's holiness: for me a church without pews is like an army general out of uniform.

The pastor was a lean, small fellow in a white short-sleeved shirt, grey trousers and a short black tie. He had a completely white head of unkempt hair, a jutting white beard and a face that was so white and pale his skin seemed to have been scalded. He had large luminous eyes which appeared to hold pools of knowledge beyond ordinary beings, as if a gift of rare vision were deliberately disguised in an unassuming human frame. But he gave a tired, distracted message about the power of Satan.

'Only about ten per cent of our community attend church on any kind of a regular basis,' the pastor said. 'The lives of about ninety per cent of Americans have been taken over by Satan. Satan has a powerful grip on our national life, on the media, on entertainment, on everything around us.'

He related the bad news in a bare, exhausted voice, unemotionally telling his listeners that the battle had been lost, like an executive of a dying company presenting a cheerless annual report to shareholders. They were, he said, surrounded on all sides by a huge evil army of unbelievable variety. They had fought a good fight, but their opponents, growing every minute, would soon reach their last defences: Satanists, homosexuals, bisexuals, transsexuals, transvestites, gangsta rappers, givers and receivers of abortions, junkies and drug merchants, two-faced politicians, greedy businessmen and stock market speculators, prostitutes, pornographers, psychics, mediums, adulterers, fornicators, and single mothers on welfare – an unstoppable typhoon of evildoing.

My own sinful mind drifted away to a life of sin and plenty: to women with flowing blonde hair racing past on the freeway in powerful jeeps, half-naked black women with exquisite breasts (the sort that model for *Ebony*), a six-figure-salary job in an office surrounded by mighty brilliant fountains, cooled by tall trees, two nice new cars parked in a sprawling bungalow of Mediterranean design on the crest of a golden brown hill overlooking a valley of jostling cypress and eucalyptus . . . Andrew nudged me awake in time for the last hymn which was led by Jenny, a plump, edgy woman in a dowdy maternity dress of faded flowers, whose shrill voice seemed to have been made only for bitter argument, certainly not for any sort of singing.

'Our pastor travelled; Tim is just standing in for him for a few weeks,' Andrew said, perhaps in apology for the sleep-inducing sermon.

The congregation descended on us the moment the service ended, shaking Andrew's hand, slapping his shoulders, making sure he was in good health, and putting in, now and again, a question about his friend. Responding to all the effusive pleasantries was clearly torturing Andrew. He had to smile broadly for everyone, nod his head repeatedly, shake all those hands and find answers to all the supposedly witty things said to him. I learnt later that this church had sponsored Andrew's trip to America to receive missionary training: he was their responsibility and every single one of them had to be assured that everything was all right with him. I stood to one side and answered such questions as were directed at me with nods and smiles, like a deaf mute, wondering how Andrew went through this every Sunday.

We finally made it to the door where the small stand-in pastor waited.

'I hope my modest effort was not too modest,' he said to us shyly.

'No, no, no,' Andrew said, 'it was a very moving message, Tim. It was very inspiring.'

'Thank you very much, Andrew,' Tim said with genuine gratitude.

Andrew introduced me to Tim as his friend visiting from Nigeria. Tim asked what I thought about California. I answered with another nod and another smile. Jenny of the dowdy dress of faded flowers appeared and gave Andrew a hug. It turned out she was Tim's wife. As soon as she heard I'd just come from Nigeria, she asked us over to their house for lunch. I looked at Andrew in desperation but saw there was nothing he could do: he was the property of the church. I'd always thought that white people didn't act so impulsively, that a lunch date was something to be agonised over by husband and wife for days, even weeks: apparently, for Andrew different rules applied.

We followed Tim and Jenny's Bronco down narrow roads that seemed like tunnels because of overhanging trees. Twice we had to get out of the way for drivers, usually in nifty-looking sports cars, speeding dangerously along those restful roads. The pastor and his wife lived in a small white house which we reached by means of a narrow track, so narrow you wouldn't see it from the road unless you were looking out for it, over a bridge of plank and steel across a little clear stream that ran over reddish-brown and off-white pebbles. The clearing resembled a set for a 1950s movie about bwanas and memsahibs in the African savannah. The house, half-covered by creepers, had a porch with two cane chairs and a low table, and I half-expected a gnarled old black man, clothed only in an ancient blanket, to emerge from one of the little outhouses and limp across the grass field to welcome Tim and Jenny and their two guests. Long shafts of sunlight, unevenly sliced by the creepers running down the tall, large windows, ornamented a large light brown sofa in the living room and a slim rug of dark red and chocolate mosaic. The room was delightfully cool and warmly welcoming at the same time. Tim might not have been the greatest preacher in America and Jenny might not have had the voice (or figure) of Whitney Houston, but their lovely home considerably redeemed them in my eyes.

While Jenny was busy in the kitchen, Tim and Andrew discussed diverse church matters – the pastor who was on vacation, the attendance which seemed to be dwindling until between them they had accounted for most people who had been absent for the last few services. Someone was away in Europe on business, some family had gone to the East Coast to spend time with relatives, poor Mrs So-and-so had not been feeling well lately, and so on. They talked at length about Andrew's course at the school for young missionaries which seemed to be nearing an end. It was as if I wasn't there at all.

The food, served in the airy, spotlessly clean kitchen, was excellent, or maybe I was just very hungry. The white fish dissolved tastily in my mouth, the roast potatoes went well with the vegetables and gravy. Everything was going very nicely from my point of view until Tim turned his scalded face towards me and asked:

'So, Obi, when did you become a born-again Christian?'

There was silence while I pondered how to tackle that question. Andrew, who had, with my silent approval, answered most of the questions meant for me, looked on helplessly.

'I'm not a born-again Christian, at least not in the sense in which I think you mean,' I said.

'Are you a born-again Christian in any sense?' Tim asked like a cross-examining lawyer, in an exasperated tone.

'I will not describe myself as a born-again Christian in any sense,' I answered in a firm voice, now determined to meet head on any challenge he might wish to pose. The escape route I had left open in my qualified answer had been as much for him as for me; he had slammed it shut by his adversarial cleverness, and, no longer interested in being a well-behaved guest, I braced myself to face him squarely. But Tim was not a fighting man. Instead, he looked at Andrew with grievously injured eyes, as if his guest had become a fifth columnist in the doomed struggle against sin, and had led one of the evildoing ninety-or-so per cent into the innermost bunkers of the faithful.

Ebullient Jenny tried to start up a conversation about Nigeria but the lunch was beyond salvage. Tim picked at his food dispiritedly, wearing a long face, and Andrew looked sick and extremely uncomfortable. Soon their low spirits infected Jenny. Perversely, I began to feel quite pleased with myself. I had one more helping of the soft white fish, two helpings of a delicious pudding that came after and drank three tall glasses of Coke and ice. I thanked Tim and Jenny for a good lunch and didn't feel particularly bad when I got a less than cheerful reply.

◆

Andrew never again invited me to church after that. But, for as long as I lived with him, I had to cope with his neo-Gandhian fundamentalist Christianity which combined a fierce devotion to God with a belief that all earthly pleasure was revolting. When he prayed at night, he remained kneeling for hours until I thought he had fallen asleep on his knees. Then a rapid staccato sound issuing from the kneeling form would tell me he had begun to pray in tongues which usually meant he was only halfway through the day's prayer. He went into days of complete fasting during which he lost weight with frightening rapidity; his meals, when he did eat, were piled with vegetables cooked to a tasteless mushiness. (I sought refuge from the tyranny of dead vegetables in Burger King and Jack-in-the-Box and Pizza Hut – my palate was the first part of me to become completely Americanised.)

Careless spending was for Andrew a brand of sinfulness, and sugar (the real one, not the substitutes), saturated fat and cholesterol were children of the devil. He shopped as though there were magnets of evil hidden in supermarket shelves. He would peer at a shelf from a safe distance for a long time then quickly reach out and grab something and step back swiftly. He would then peer at the can or packet, adjusting his thick glasses, his lips moving slowly as he analysed the nutritional information. This process would be repeated for all the things he had to buy that day. I went to Safeway on Grand Avenue with him once and that was quite enough for me. The best liquid in the world was, of course, water – the one that flowed from the tap not the type spendthrift Americans wasted money buying from the shops. Orange juice and diet soft drinks he kept only for visitors. And whenever I ate Haagen Daz's Bailey's Irish Cream ice cream (to which I quickly became addicted) in his presence, his eyes made me feel as though I were engaged in fornication.

From Robo, who had had phases of religiousness, I knew another variant of born-again Christianity – one in which pretty girls, dressed in the latest fashions, swayed to computer-assisted music in brightly lit, colourful Lagos churches; in which those pretty girls could have sex with their boyfriends early on Sunday morning, after hours of frenzied dancing in a nightclub all Saturday night, and still manage to get up groggily and rush to church on Sunday morning and not feel too guilty because they planned to marry the boyfriends anyway, which in their minds qualified them to do the things married couples were allowed to do by the Bible. (Of course, you didn't know if your boyfriend also planned to marry *you*, even when he said he did, since men were jerks, but you hoped for the best and put your faith in the

Lord.) Andrew's faith permitted no such compromises, no creative, self-serving interpretations of the scriptures; every little grain of earthly pleasure was a deadly poison and had to be kept many miles away. He had been very religious at university, but I noticed a new ferocity in his faith which I put down to America: that intensified, uncompromising neo-Gandhian Christianity was his defence against this nation of countless easy, potentially fatal pleasures from hamburgers to anal sex.

◆

I discovered Berkeley while waiting for the forged documents which would enable me to look for a job and quickly took to the university city of bookshops and cafés. The first time I encountered Telegraph Street was on a sunny afternoon in mid-August. It was gloriously crowded with Maori, Red Indian, Rastafarian and thirty-years-late hippie hairstyles, Hell's Angels leather jackets, Bedouin and Confucian robes, US Marine fatigues and many kinds of near-nudity, big colourful ear- and noserings, bangles and beads. In a light blue shirt and khaki pants, I felt odd.

I stopped by the tabletop shops which sold beads and cheap batik and I bought things I didn't need. I stared at posters calling for demonstrations against Newt Gingrich's 'Contract on America' and the enemies of affirmative action, denouncing Jesse Helms, Clarence Thomas, Deng Xiao-Ping and the Iranian mullahs; posters offering French and Spanish lessons, beginner and advanced, pets for adoption, 'sweet room-mates' with long lists of likes and dislikes, and intimate massages at bargain prices. I sat in cafés and scalded my tongue with hot coffee, pretending to be reading while listening to the talk all around me, about all the things in this world: sex, politics, religion, music, lousy teachers, money problems. I imagined myself sometime in the future, a graduate student, engaging in these conversations instead of eavesdropping.

Leaning against the side of a building, or through the door or window of a café, I stared at passing young women for hours with shameless lust, their bare midriffs, their long bare legs, their fresh faces. The Asian girls had the greatest effect on me. They looked younger than everyone else, perhaps because they were often smaller. Their colour set them apart, even though they knew what coffees and bagels to order, what jokes to tell and laugh at and, as far as I could see, worked the ATMs expertly. Through Hollywood I'd become familiar with black and white American women back in Nigeria, but I couldn't remember any significant Asian character in the films I had seen. So lust for the exotic welled up inside me whenever a Japanese or Chinese girl passed nearby, and an invisible hand brushed lightly over my crotch.

It was inevitable that one day I would go from lustful staring to seduction. The moment came one afternoon in Cody's Book-shop. I was leafing through novels at random and nearly fell over a figure seated on the tiled floor between two shelves, back against the wall, legs in a lotus position, head bowed low so the long brown hair almost touched the floor, like a devotee of an eastern religion in an attitude of meditation. She looked up as I stood staring at her – staring at women had become a habit I fell into unconsciously – and I saw she'd been reading a book which lay in the hollow formed by her legs.

'Hi,' I said and smiled to cover up my embarrassment.

'Hi,' she said, her eyes puzzled.

She wasn't Chinese or Japanese and was rather plain, with an acne jaw, but I reminded myself that I wasn't in a position to be too picky. There was a long silence while I racked my brain for an opening line.

'I'm new around here, and I'm still trying to get to know the bookshops – *and* the people,' I said finally, feeling I hadn't done too badly considering the suddenness.

'What was that?' she asked, still looking very puzzled as if I was a mad-looking man who had just wandered into her home.

'I'm new,' I said again, 'I've just come from Africa.'

'Oh, you are new, and you are from Africa. That explains the accent,' she said and waited for me to go on.

'For a while I thought you were praying or something,' I said.

'What did you say?' she asked again with that same puzzled look.

'I said I thought for a moment that you were praying,' I repeated, pronouncing each word slowly and distinctly like someone speaking to an idiot.

'Oh, you thought for a moment that I was praying,' she repeated, also speaking the words slowly, pronouncing each of them carefully in her American accent, rescuing them, like abused children, from the violence my accent had done to them.

The spoken Englishes of Africa, heavily overlaid with the intonations of indigenous languages, can be difficult to cope with, but I'd always thought my accent was one of the better ones. My father, a graduate of classics and a teacher of literature before he became a civil servant, had made sure I learnt English before I began to speak Igbo, in order to prepare me for the world. I'd grown up in a house full of books and was well acquainted with Dickens and Hardy, Hemingway and Capote, Achebe and Baldwin, so it was terribly galling to be made to feel as though I spoke with a mouth full of water. I realised with time that the often hilarious efforts of some of my fellow immigrant countrymen and women to sound American had nothing to do with affectation; it was a matter of survival – to many American ears a foreign accent was off-putting, like a bad smell.

My first attempt at seduction drowned in the gulf between my accent and that of the girl with long brown hair. I retreated in embarrassment and frustration, remembering something I'd read somewhere: that the Americans and the British are people divided by the same language and I thought how that statement applied even more accurately to the Third World bastard-offspring of the former British Empire. I felt the girl's eyes following me, still very puzzled.

Like almost everyone else in the world, I'd heard that American women, next only to the Scandinavians, were sexually liberal and exciting and I'd looked forward to a career of debauchery in America, at least until Robo came over. I had hoped that 'I'm new, I've just come from Africa' would provoke immediate interest in young, lively minds upon which I would then build. Instead, my foreignness felt like a crippled leg. I never again found the courage to attempt seduction during those days of hanging around Berkeley; I just lurked and stared and hungered.

The Warehouses of Despair

After I had acquired my forged social security card, it took me another two weeks to get a job. You didn't just wave dodgy papers at anyone and ask for work; there were illegal-friendly employers and there were certain channels through which they were contacted. The illegal was like a rat subsisting in the sewers of a large city: ignoring the right channels could spell doom. Andrew knew someone who knew someone else, a Nigerian who had lived in Oakland for a long time who was a sort of one-man labour agency for illegals. Andrew made the contact and two weeks later I got a call to go and see a Mrs Beth Elgassier at an office on Grand Avenue to be interviewed for a job (the caller didn't say what kind of job it was). If I got the job I was to give Andrew one hundred dollars immediately to give to the someone he knew for the caller; when I received my first salary, I was to pay another hundred dollars by the same procedure. It all sounded rather sinister, like espionage, and I went to see Mrs Elgassier full of misgivings.

The office looked straight at the stately old Grand Lake movie theatre whose front, shaped like one half of a tall wedding cake, jutted out towards the street; the sign above the door of the office said: Bay Area Corporate Security. There were three desks, only one of which was occupied, and a plain brown carpet. From the name I'd naively expected a fellow foreigner, someone from Turkey, Greece or a place like that but found that Beth Elgassier in looks and in accent was unimpeachably American. She looked mid- or late fifties: some wrinkles had arrived but they were still gentle, and there remained a hint of the good looks she must have had when she was younger. When she stood up to shake my hand and offer me a seat, I noticed that she was tall for a woman, about my height, five eleven, and had a lean body, including a chest as flat as a blackboard. She was dressed in a smart gold-coloured waistcoat, a white long-sleeved shirt and black pants; she wore a thin gold chain, her perfume filled the long office, and she had a bright, youthful smile. I was grateful for that smile; I'd seen nothing resembling a smile in weeks. She let me know immediately that she was not Mrs but Miss, and told me that Al was not around and that I would have to wait for about thirty minutes or come back later; I chose to wait for Al, whoever he was.

'You're Nigerian, I hear. Long way from home.'

I nodded.

Now that I knew I had a problematic accent, it was wise to say as little as possible.

'Do you like it so far?' she asked.

'Yes, it's beautiful.'

'You like the weather?'

'Yes, very much.'

'This is a good time. I love the summer months though some people complain that it gets too hot. You went to college in Nigeria?'

'Yes.'

'We get many Nigerians and they all have college degrees. Do a lot of people have college degrees in Nigeria?'

'Yes, quite a lot.'

We chatted for a long time, or rather she talked for a long time and I listened and answered when I had to in a few words. She told me which movies I should go and watch, and that Oakland was not a bad place to live in but people who didn't live here heard about the crime and violence in a few areas on TV and wrote the whole city off. She asked me about my family and told me that she had a daughter from a broken marriage, who was in the US army and lived on an army base in Germany.

Mozer – I can never bring myself to think of him as Al – came in while I was laughing at something Ms Elgassier had said, and his collapsed, sick and tired face made me feel I had been indulging in unpardonable levity. His stomach navigated for the rest of him; he seemed to be suffering from excruciating pain in his back which he tried to reduce by walking stomach-first in a quick pre-programmed manner. He wore a crumpled brown suit and white shirt and a crumpled plain brown tie; he was himself quite crumpled. Ms Elgassier introduced me. I smiled at Mozer and greeted him. He looked me over and answered the greeting grudgingly: pleasantness in this office was clearly Ms Elgassier's responsibility, not his.

Mozer showed me into an inner office which I hadn't noticed before because its door was of the same colour as the cream wall of the outer office. He sat behind the desk in a leather swivel chair that was too big for his small body and I sat opposite him.

'I've had many Nigerians here before. Some of them gave me a lot of trouble, got into some criminal stuff, but I'm not going to hold it against you. I'm a fair man; I give everyone a chance, and I'll give you a chance.' The words trickled out of him like water from a leaky pipe.

You hear while you live in Nigeria about the notoriety of your fellow citizens abroad, but you never quite feel it fully until you leave the country; it is like a suitcase which looks heavy but, when you have to lift it, you discover is even heavier than it appeared. On my first trip outside Nigeria, to London in 1992, Immigration at Gatwick was slow and bloody-minded: every speck on the notorious green passport was considered suspicious and had to be explained to sceptical eyes. And for that flight their vigilance was rewarded – they bagged a frail-looking young man whose British visa was forged. His pathetic denials – I swear to almighty God, I receive that visa from Mr Wilson of British Embassy Marina Lagos; I swear to almighty God, you can phone Mr Wilson now-now and ask him – reached my ears as I stood in front of the lady immigration officer who was examining my own passport. I kept my eyes fixed on the lady's pretty Indian features, as if turning to look at the frail-looking man would immediately establish the existence of a conspiracy between him and myself.

Mozer's eyes watched my face closely as he spoke. Those eyes seemed certain that I was both a drug dealer and a con artist and the job he was offering me was a trap to catch me. As I'd begun to suspect when I saw the sign outside the office, I was to work as a security guard.

'I want you at work on time. I don't want complaints from the other guys about your attitude. I got a lot of those about the Nigerians who worked here before. They had been to college back in Nigeria and they thought they were too important for the job, but they were not too important for the pay.'

51

I nodded. I'd been holding my degree in economics in reserve, waiting for an opening to play that card – even if I was going to do a menial job, I hoped I'd get a little extra for doing it with a degree – but I saw at that moment that, if anything, a university degree was a liability here.

Ms Elgassier was to help me fill the forms and do some of the other formal stuff. I was to begin the next day as a trainee, join the others and see how it was done; I would get on the regular schedule after a week. The hours for my first month would be eleven p.m. to seven a.m., I'd get one free night a week, and the pay would be seven dollars an hour.

'Any questions?'

I didn't have any.

◆

I soon learnt that when Mozer said something was going to last for a month it usually went on for the rest of your life unless you changed it somehow. I was assigned – for my first month, Mozer said – to a compound of two huge, weathered warehouses just off 98th Street, beside Interstate 880 South. My partner on the first night had been there for five years and he, too, had been told at the beginning that he was being assigned to the warehouses for his first month. His name was Maina, a Kenyan who had dropped out of Cal State Hayward with only a year to getting his degree.

Maina said his father had been an important politician in Kenya – later Maina said it was his uncle who had been an important politician and later still he said his father was a poor farmer who had suffered all his life – anyway, someone had been an important politician and had paid Maina's fees right through school in Kenya and then at Cal State. Whoever it was had fallen out of favour with the Kenyan president in the early '90s for reasons that were not very clear. In an early version of the story it sounded as though that someone had been unable to continue paying Maina's fees after his political problems began, but in later versions it emerged that Maina had not dropped out for financial reasons but because he could no longer concentrate on his studies, for worrying about his sponsor's political problems and the problems of Kenya and Africa at large (maybe even of the whole world), or (maybe or/and) because he wanted to go into business and make a lot of money; he didn't want a middle class life oppressed by mortgage payments and bills.

The security guard job was just to make ends meet while his companies stabilised: he was involved in, or going to be involved in, importing tea from Kenya into America. He was rendering, or hoped to render, consultancy services to American companies planning to do business in Kenya and in other parts of Africa. He was also negotiating, or dreaming of, the construction of a hotel/shopping centre/amusement park complex in the tourist city of Mombasa, on the Indian Ocean. He came to work on some nights with a bundle of files and took over one of the two desks in the guards' office, poring over the papers with inhuman concentration. If I came near him he would brusquely shut the files and glare at me.

He confided to me that they contained business secrets – proposals, minutes of meetings, confidential studies, those sort of things. He proudly showed me the business cards and letterhead papers of his many companies: Maina Impex Inc., Maina Mombasa Dev. Consortium Inc., Maina Processing Inc. and so on. He showed me letters to businessmen, invariably with powerful-sounding names – Wallerstein, Waldhortz, Skiff – making series of proposals, seeking meetings, guaranteeing unbelievable profit margins, but he never showed me any replies. He assured me, though, that things were moving along very well, interest had been expressed, more documentation requested, for you know how it is with these extremely rich men, very cautious, very, very cautious. The breakthrough deal was only a hair's breadth away, always just a whisker away, just a phone call away, one more letter, one single document awaited from business partners in Kenya and then the promised land: a huge office, state-of-the-art furnishing, first class travel, designer suits, in a word, Paradise. He told me I was under probation – I looked like a serious, trustworthy individual, unlike other Nigerians he had met who were frivolous and dishonest. If I didn't do anything to spoil the positive impression he had of me, once things stabilised in any of his businesses, we would leave the wretched security guard work together and begin to make real money: he wouldn't think of employing an American manager when there were intelligent African brothers forced to do menial jobs. He knew the exact spot in the Oakland Hills where he would build his house – these American houses were not good enough; he would design his own and get a construction company to build it to his specifications. All that remained was that cruelly elusive breakthrough deal that was always just a whisker away . . .

For all his hatred of frivolity and his business-driven single-mindedness, Maina felt he had to relate to me his many sexual adventures. His life seemed to consist of two equal parts: one was concerned with forming companies and planning how to make millions of dollars, the other did nothing but sleep with women of diverse races, and since I was his African brother he could not hold back from telling me about those women. It was a useless life to lead, of course, and he advised me strongly against following in his footsteps, but he was already trapped. He could do nothing about all the women who demanded sex from him on a daily basis. To me he didn't sound trapped, though; rather he told of his alleged escapades with crazy happiness. He seemed intoxicated by his own tales, dependent on them, like an alcoholic.

He said he had three steady girlfriends – Letitia, an African-American girl, the most beautiful African-American girl in Oakland, she would easily win the Miss America competition if she entered, but she was from a good home and was serious-minded, and serious-minded people didn't do such things. On some days Letitia became Patricia or Phyllis, but whatever name she took on she remained one of the most beautiful black women in the world. There was a Seminole Indian, Ruth (or Beatrice), who was also incredibly beautiful. Red Indians had to be the most beautiful women in the world with dreamy eyes and wonderful noses, and their bodies (*Oh My God!*). And then there was a tiny Korean woman, whose names of two or three letters changed so many times that I lost track. She was so tiny you could scoop her up with one hand like a chick just emerging from an egg, and also, of course, incredibly beautiful. These three ravishingly beautiful women and many others too numerous to mention were engaged in a life and death struggle for Maina (a big, ungainly fellow with a long, repulsive head and a nose like an elephant's trunk), or more accurately for the extraordinary size of his penis and brilliant sex styles which made him (by his own reckoning) probably the most sought-after stud on the west coast of the United States.

Women with sharp jutting breasts, narrow bottomless eyes, slender powdered noses walked up to Maina in bars and nightclubs, drawn by the magnets in his eyes. They followed him to his apartment only minutes later, poured wine all over his ungainly body and licked it up slowly (oh! so slowly he thought he would die, so unbearable he cried like a little baby), and had sex with him so many times they left him sore but delirious. The same women floated across the vast plains around our warehouses, where the silence was only interrupted by airplanes landing at or taking off from the nearby Oakland airport, above the airline hangars huge like stomachs distended by kwashiorkor, to suck Maina's nipples, to assault his body with their silken fingers until he began to writhe helplessly in our guards' room that smelt thickly of all the greasy food that had passed through the old microwave oven.

I had been working at the warehouses for three weeks, had almost become as dependent as Maina on his tales, when I encountered his other side.

'Brother,' I greeted him cheerily as I got into the guards' room one night (that was the greeting he'd insisted on), 'what's been happening to you?' (usually the trigger for the day's tales).

He gave me the look of a terrible enemy, of someone who would like nothing better than to cut me to pieces. His lips quivered, his eyes, bloated and bloodshot, were fixed on me unblinkingly, filled with hatred. Only the day before Maina had been telling me of a nice letter from one of the rich men with powerful names he was trying to interest in investing in Kenya. He had left work in buoyant spirits. The man who smouldered on the desk in front of me was so different from the cheerful fellow I had parted from the day before I wondered if it was Maina at all.

'Anything the matter?' I asked.

Maina cocked his cucumber head to one side and sneered at me. A complicated coughing, grunting, expectorating sound rose from within him and I was scared for a moment that he would fire a big glob of phlegm into my face. He swallowed noisily, turned to me fiercely as though I had just killed his mother and he was about to kill me in revenge, and hissed something terrible, then he turned away from me to stare at the small notice-board crammed with duty schedules, newspaper cuttings and dry jokes. Imagine a night of that – eight hours of grunting, coughing, hissing, glaring, of a bitter silence swollen with inexplicable hatred; imagine the steady drumming of my heart all through that first night, for I was sure Maina had lost his mind and I didn't know how far he would go. I never turned my back on him that night; when I looked at the novel I was reading, I couldn't make sense of the words. My stomach was tense, the room was suffocating.

Maina hissed things, snarled without warning: 'You think you are clever. You want to be a slave, nothing more. Sit behind a desk; wear a nasty tie. MBA, my foot. Your MBA will only be good for toilet paper. You want to be successful, American dollar in your pocket, but you are just a fool. You'll see for yourself that it's all a trick.'

I'd told him I hoped to go to graduate school one day and get an MBA, but I soon deduced that he was not just hissing at me but at a large audience upon which his hate-filled eyes focused unblinkingly, an audience of which I was only just a little part. His bitterness was directed against all forms of ambition, all variants of the American dream. I would find out later, I would suffer, all my dreams would be in vain, it was a trick, I aspired only to be a slave, I was doomed, we were all doomed, all those running after MBAs and the American dollar. Out of him poured fumes, warnings of disaster.

'I shared a place with one of your Nigerians,' he hissed on one of those nights. 'He thought he was going to be the next immigrant multibillionaire. Full of himself, the bastard. Social climber, party animal, ass licker. The women loved him, he said. He was on his way to the top, they would help to take him there. He moved in with a girl whose father was a big shot. They attended all the parties, went to the fucking Golden Gate Theatre to see the fucking musicals, black tie dinners. He wore the latest sunglasses, real sophisticated asshole. Drove around in the girl-friend's sportscar. All-American immigrant. The fool married her, then, yes, he got his good job with a big company, bought his own sportscar. Two years after, she threw him out; she was bored. She threw him out and kept everything. He couldn't believe it, he was in love with her, he couldn't bear to be without her. He began to hear voices, started talking to himself. Shock was too much for the poor fool. He's now in a madhouse in South San Francisco. I went to see him. Not out of sympathy, I have no sympathy for fools. I warned him, I know this country, and I warned him but he wouldn't listen. I went to see him at the madhouse just to amuse myself. Saliva was coming out of the corners of his mouth, when he saw me he started crying. It was so funny, oh so funny, the stupid bastard.'

In time I began to find Maina's grunting and hissing and his glares of hatred irritating and tedious, like having to watch a poorly acted play again and again. People had all sorts of loads to carry in this world and he was just not carrying his own very well. He'd dropped out of school, had no hopes of middle-class success of his own so he turned with venom on what he had lost; basic, boring sour grapes. Tales of breakthrough deals which were always only a hair's breadth away and his myriad ravenous sexual partners were suppressants, but now and again that acidic bitterness completely seized him and turned him into a vicious, grunting, glaring animal. But all this analysis came several weeks after that first night. In the early days Maina's mood swings kept me off balance. I went to work nervous, unsure whether it would be business deals or wanton sex or hisses and abuse. I had nightmares about Maina's nameless Nigerian room-mate, who assumed the form of close friends from school, most often my own room-mate, Bronzo, slimy white stuff dribbling from the corners of his mouth, his eyes large and wild, floating in a pool of madness. I dreamt of Maina himself, armed with a machete chasing me down Grand Avenue at night while people passing in cars laughed, thinking that two black men were merely enjoying a wild but harmless joke.

Maina occasionally worked daytime shifts (after a few years with the firm, you became entitled to do day and night shifts alternately, but there were no clear rules, everything depended on Mozer), and other people joined me at night. These were mainly transients, who worked on average for four weeks and moved on.

Fung was a short, fat Chinese man of about sixty, so short-sighted that even with his glasses on he still collided into things. That a man who could hardly see anything more than two feet away from him could be employed as a security guard suggested to me that our job was not to secure anything but to report for work every night, fill the bulky ledger with cryptic remarks like 'Patrolled perimeter 12.00 p.m., No Incident' and go to the office every fortnight for our wages and listen to the talkative Ms Elgassier. Our only real challenge was surviving boredom.

Fung's troubles could easily fill the warehouses under our charge and they got more twisted every day. His three daughters were smart and hardworking but perennially unlucky in love. Rakes, womanisers, givers of bad cheques, crooks of every kind promised them the world then promptly took their money and broke their hearts. Falling in love was probably as nice as it was made out to be, Fung said, but what was the use if only a few months after you were left in pain, you had to be kept away from sleeping pills, you ran high temperatures and doctors had to be summoned in the middle of the night? Seeing as it brought so much suffering, what was the use of it? Why was so much made by Americans of something which brought so much pain? They should be warning people against love, Fung, weary dis-traught father, said, not pushing them into it. There should be large billboards on the streets, commercials on prime time tele-vision, films about it, newspaper columns, pendants, buttons, banners warning against love, pressure groups campaigning against it.

And on top of all that, Fung's landlord increased his rent all the time, and he hated making trouble so he just went ahead and paid which encouraged the landlord to increase the rent further. So Fung, not wanting any trouble, looked for money and paid, and then the predator would increase the rent further, and Fung would pay, and so it went on. And Fung's health was showing signs of wear: he'd been treated for kidney problems and he wouldn't have minded dying right away except that his two youngest children were doing well in school and he wanted to be able to go on supporting them. And there were money troubles all the time, the struggle every month to pay the ever rising rent, things to be bought for the children, utility bills that arrived with unpleasant punctuality.

It was somewhat comforting, in this age when you keep running into comparisons between Asian tigers and African laggards, to find an Asian who was not developing or bootlegging new software or managing billion dollar investments, but was hopelessly thrashing about in a bog of failure; whose daughters were not precocious superwomen or specialists in some rare branch of medicine, but were regular young women slowly and painfully learning the lessons of love and pain as we all must. Fung's troubles pursued him even while he slept (it was of course against the rules to sleep on duty, but you had to be exceptionally cruel to think of making a report against that helpless old man), and in between his snores, a furious argument in some Chinese tongue clattered out of him like an old typewriter.

Mahamood, a little, lean, restless, talkative man, who joined the firm two months after I did, was obsessed with spiritual matters. America's problems were all traceable to the spirit. Political and economic struggles were a waste of time.

'Those are the *symptoms*, not the *cause*,' Mahamood declared. 'You first got to fix the spirit; if you don't fix the spirit you're wasting a whole load of energy. You know what I'm saying?'

I didn't know what he was saying, and after listening to his unwieldy mix of theories and faiths, the bits and pieces of superstition and brainwave which he had collected over time the way a river collects rubbish, I became convinced that he didn't either. An African-American priestess of the gads-af-Africa (he said it like one word) – in fact it wasn't correct to call her an African-American woman at all because she had become, after the things that had happened to her, a complete African, the only thing American about her was her passport, jes that little book for travelin' – that priestess had opened his eyes.

He had seen her one evening in a bar on 14th Street and he'd gone up to her trying to talk some sex out of her – before his conversion he had been mad about sex. She had listened to his lines and had shaken her head in sorrow at what was happening to a strong African-American male like him. Then she had sat him down and told him things which set him on the right path. The crux of her powerful message was this: man would only regain his place in the world when he regained *harmony* with the *forces* that had brought him into the world. Since that revelation his life had not been the same; he had rejected the *shallowness* of human existence, and he was embarked on a journey to the spiritual origins of mankind.

It sounded like an epic, Arabian Nights kind of quest: over forbidding mountains, past the edges of terrible cliffs, through valleys crawling with serpents and scorpions, to treasures hidden in the nostrils of the gods, but all that the journey had turned up so far were pieces of ancestor-worship, stuff from the Ten Commandments, astral and extra-terrestrial travel, ESP, Progression through Spheres of Righteousness to a Position of Oneness with the Chosen Ones, the gods of Yorubaland and Dahomey as reborn in Haiti and Cuba, UFOs, secret research at NASA on life in outer space, the work of mediums, the existence of evil beings in various parts of the Atlantic and the Pacific, etc. etc. Revealed to me in the numbing boredom of the guards' room as astonishing, original discoveries.

One night, when I was feeling irritable, I told him that gods and all that were not really my priority at the time; all I wanted was a good job, the ability to buy a few creature comforts. I wasn't spiritual and it was very unlikely I would ever be. Mahamood went crazy. He hopped about like a monkey, his pupils dilated, his dark face in torment, shrieking that the white man had got my brain, oh yeah, mashed it up like mashed potato and served it up for himself on a plate, oh yeah, the white man had stuck a great big cassette into my brain full of the white man's godless lies and I jes went on playing that white man's cassette with my lips, like a cassette player. He seized *The Satanic Verses*, which I was reading for the fourth time, and held it up as evidence of what the white man had done to my brain, reading evil books by evil white people, filling my head with the white man's trash, oh he wasn't angry with me, no way he would get angry, he just *pitied* my ass. I was very worried that he would do severe injury to *The Satanic Verses*, but fortunately when his seizure subsided, he merely brought the book down gently on the desk.

Before Mahamood left to continue his epic spiritual journey, after two pay cheques, he looked at me with pity and warned me one last time to be wary of the white man's books and the white man's lies, otherwise the man would suck me dry and throw me away like a dry orange.

I remember the Romanian actor, Ionesco, almost with affection. He was tall and spindly, had a sweet, effeminate voice. He tried very hard to sound American, but a rich European strain of English that suggested ageless Gothic cathedrals and professors of abstract philosophies in universities nearly older than mankind, clung to him tenaciously like the smell of onions. Thick red hair sprouted from every part of him like an overgrown shrub, and his breath perpetually had a faint whiff of marijuana. He had come to the Bay Area from the East Coast looking for work as a stage actor; he had suffered discrimination back there, he said, because he was European, especially an East European, and someone had told him that there were more open-minded acting companies in California. By the time Ionesco came to work at the warehouses, he had been around here for ten months and the nearest he had come to acting in a play was moving the furniture about between scenes in a production of Harold Pinter's *Betrayal* at the Durham Theatre in Berkeley. He was close to despair.

Because I asked him if he was related to the playwright Eugene Ionesco (he wasn't), and because he saw me reading a novel the first day we met, he embraced me as a fellow man of Culture; an Enlightened Being. He recited acres of Shakespeare to me in his soothing voice, and brought back memories of listening to my father's stories from Shakespeare's plays, interspersed with quotations, when I was about seven, before the civil service swallowed him like quicksand, so that by the time I read Lamb's *Tales from Shakespeare* in secondary school, I was convinced I knew more Shakespeare than our literature teacher. I have a porous mind and can't memorize more than two lines of anything, and I was astounded by the hundreds of lines that Ionesco delivered with ease as we stood outside in the cold night air. His voice and the red and yellow lights on the freeway at the end of a row of warehouses bore my mind away from my seedy surroundings. But hearing that stubborn accent bumping into words now and again, like a car going over potholes, I saw why he stood little chance of getting into an English language play in the Bay Area or elsewhere (except perhaps Romania).

There was a Camerounian who hated Nigerians and told me to my face that *all* Nigerians were thieves, con men, promiscuous, irresponsible, indisciplinable, spendthrift, etc. When he was thrown out of the house he shared with another Camerounian, for his obnoxiousness I was sure, all Camerounians became dishonest, wicked, inconsiderate and so on. There was a Nigerian employee who was assigned to work elsewhere but whom I sometimes met at the office on pay days. The thin malnourished fellow with frightened eyes would quickly walk over immediately he saw me, shake my hand very firmly, and ask after my health. When he heard I was doing fine, he would quickly pull back to a corner of the room and, his duty to a fellow countryman done, bury his face in a newspaper.

◆

Night work stood my world on its head. I made my way to the warehouses, with a novel and a brown bag of two burgers, fries (large), two sodas, in an old thick sweater (as it was beginning to get cold at night), long after downtown Oakland had been emptied of workers; and I went back home on cold early mornings as people who led normal lives were getting ready to leave for work. Even when at university the terror of approaching exams drove last minute crashers to study all night, I had never studied past midnight, being a strong believer in the law of diminishing returns. I had only remained awake far into the night at nightclubs or parties or to read a novel I couldn't put down or when pushed to a peak of sexual excitement and performance by a girl I'd just met or hadn't slept with in a long time.

It took me about two hours to get to sleep after work, and I would usually wake up at about four p.m., spend one more hour in bed, tired, lethargic and despondent, then I would call myself a lazy, sulking, self-pitying bastard and force my body off the bed. By the time I had had a bath and dressed, I would have about only one and a half hours to get my hamburgers and fries and catch a bus to work. Mozer took not eight but twenty-four hours of my life every work day.

I silently joined a fraternity of night workers. I saw them on the buses early every morning, their dispirited eyes looking through the window or staring at the floor as though they could not bear to look at one another, perhaps for fear that they would see their despair reflected too clearly on other faces. We heard them at night on our small radio in the guards' office asking the San Francisco radio station that played only love songs for a Barry White or Anita Baker song to be played for Mary or Yolanda, to let her know I love her very much and I'm thinking of her every minute I spend here at work.

And the depression and tedium of those warehouses, and of our guards' office in which too much despair had congealed over time, and the blue and black uniform I wore like a badge of shame, and the freaks and drifters with whom I shared that bleak life, began to graft on me a tough coating of hopelessness. Minutes sluggishly became hours, hours days, days weeks.

I looked forward to the phone calls I made to Robo at least once every week even though the cost was punishing. I told her I was a supervisor in a security firm, doing a lot of boring paperwork, preparing workers' schedules, that sort of thing. She laughed when I told her about Fung and his daughters and Maina and his companies, but she also said she was terribly lonely and was feeling wretched, and then she always promptly blamed herself for being so feeble. My mother installed a phone in her shop in Yaba as she had sworn she would. It took five weeks, which for Lagos was near to miraculous. I spoke to them every fortnight – herself, my father and my sisters, Adaku and Nwaka. My parents kept telling me over the phone how much they were praying for me every day, as though my soul were in purgatory and needed to be diligently prayed into heaven. Adaku, whose five-year-old marriage was being buffeted by poverty, reminded me every chance she got of how hard things were. She apologised every fortnight for not being at the airport the day I left: her baby, the one that was always sick, had developed an upset tummy that evening; she too was praying hard for me. Nwaka sometimes tried to inject a cheerful note, saying she hoped I was having a good time and had met some *nice* people, but hers was a tiny flicker of candlelight in that immense darkness.

Andrew suggested I get another job as my wages from one job would not be enough to save on; I looked at him as if he had lost his mind. Maina added a girl from Norway to his list of steady girlfriends – she was on a students' exchange programme at Berkeley. Her name was Olga but it later became Frieda and later still Helga. His numerous companies remained unstable. Mozer seemed surprised that the other Nigerian and myself had not got ourselves sacked for some criminal conduct or by being uppity about our degrees. I spent my one free day a week at home, reading a novel or just lying around, surrounded by Andrew's religious posters which promised a glorious life elsewhere. And my own life seeped away like blood.

Gorilla Millionaire

When in August 1991, I told my father that I was leaving the job in CDB, a venerable old bank with a hundred branches all over Nigeria, into which he had plonked me after national service through his connections, to join a small new finance company, he was horrified. It was like abandoning a solid and tested home to go and live in a flimsy, shiny zinc shack by the roadside, he said. In CDB I would retire with a pension (and grey hairs and a bent back) after thirty-five years of faithful service, whereas these showy, one-branch finance companies and banks were all going to be blown away in no time. How could I even think of doing something so stupid? He was, I decided, suffering from colonial hangover and civil service gradualism. The British had made his generation cautious to the point of timidity; the civil service had worsened it by making life seem like a journey of a thousand slow motion steps through grades and mini-grades and fixed promotion waiting periods and hierarchies set in stone.

The new chic banks and finance companies, which were blossoming like water hyacinths all over Lagos as a result of our latest military government's pseudo-free-market economic policies, were the direct opposite of the dead civil service. They were spawning a new tribe of confident, aggressive, sharp-dressing, young bankers, and filling the roads with brand new Nissan, Honda, Toyota, Hyundai and Daewoo office cars. One of the new banks put a piano player in its banking hall; another offered hot doughnuts and coffee to customers. They paid much higher interest rates than the old banks and rendered efficient and courteous service in swanky surroundings to a people for whom going to the bank had always been as dehumanising as trying to get something done in a government ministry. It was nothing short of a revolution.

Philip, who gave me the new job, had been my senior by three years at university. His parents, like mine, lived in Yaba, and we had become friends. He had worked in a bank for five years and risen to be assistant manager, foreign exchange. While at the bank he had made a lot of money. Foreign currency was so hungrily sought after and our poor, diarrhoeal naira so thoroughly despised that it was impossible not to grow very rich from kickbacks if you worked in foreign exchange. He now wanted an outfit of his own which would evolve into a fully-fledged bank.

The finance company's office was on the top floor of a three-storied building in Victoria Island Annex, on land from which dwellers of the Maroko shanty town had been unceremoniously evicted, the way the old apartheid regime had erased black townships in South Africa. (Only that this was done by a government of black people to other black people.) The land stolen at gunpoint was at that time rapidly sprouting new office buildings and residences in a mélange of architectural styles, some beautiful, many quite hideous. Ours was one of the ugliest: a brutish concrete structure, short on ventilation and lighting and long on vulgar decorative nonsense. It had shapeless murals of brightly coloured beads libellously intended to be an example of African culture, multi-coloured and flowered wall and floor tiles and a screamingly bright red roof. It was as though the architect had played a practical joke at the owner's expense. Philip had the interior of the part of the building we occupied done in only sober colours as though to dissociate the finance company from the surrounding vulgarity. The partitioning and the wall-to-wall carpet were both in a cool golden brown, the desks were ebony. He called it Baobab Trust Finance House, BTF for short.

Philip was well built and a fast talker. He was a driven man; sparks of limitless ambition flew off his big eyeballs. Hardly had the finance company begun than he started pursuing approval to start a mortgage bank and an equipment leasing company. He inundated us with pep talks: 'We have to be highly competitive and extremely aggressive. Our watchwords must be competition, aggression, innovation. One hundred per cent is not good enough, even one hundred and fifty per cent performance is too poor. I want two hundred per cent performance at all times.' And as though the fierceness of his driven eyes was not enough, his muscular arms struck the air furiously to buttress each point, like Goebbels leading a rally. His suits were Nino Cerutti and Canali; his ties were Gianfranco Ferre and Karl Lagerfeld; his fragrances were Yves Saint Laurent and Calvin Klein; he was a world away from the rest of us.

There were three of us in Treasury and Marketing. Yemisi had worked like me in an old generation bank. Her face wasn't fantastic, but she had a figure of exciting proportions and long, beautiful legs. When she wore her near-minis, just long enough to pass as office wear but short enough to display quite a bit of brown thigh, it was difficult to pay attention to work. Amina was pretty and very light-skinned (she had an Egyptian mother and a Nigerian father), not too tall and a little plump. She didn't have any financial industry experience and didn't seem to want any. She came to work to read the *National Enquirer* and *The Sun*, *Prime People* and *Vintage People*. She was more interested in who that Fergie was sleeping with and if Ojukwu was going to finally marry Bianca than in BTF's mundane paperwork. Yemisi told me that she was sleeping with one of the members of the board and, later on – perhaps to doubly secure her job – she also started sleeping with Philip. After that she came to work only when she felt like it and never before ten a.m. So, really, Treasury and Marketing was just Yemisi and myself.

On us fell the burden of mobilising deposits, which Operations was to invest in various ventures. There were two messengers, one receptionist and two secretaries, but everyone had a p.c. and we were required to take computer classes and do most of our secretarial work ourselves. There was a car pool of two new white Nissan Sunnys and two drivers. Philip had a Honda Accord and driver to himself. There was a satellite dish, and TVs in every room, permanently tuned to CNN. The gentle patter of brand new computer keyboards, the serious-faced, serious-dress-ing, fast-talking, fast-walking young men and women sweeping in and out of offices like strong winds, filled me with energy. Fashionable words and phrases – 'strategizing', 'intermediation', 'critical success factors (csfs)', 'key performance indicators (kpis)' – leapt out of our mouths at the slightest provocation and sometimes without any provocation at all. High-tech computer graphics on CNN a few feet away from my desk analysed stock markets from New York to Hong Kong. I started as senior treasury officer, earning double what I had been paid at CDB. I was twenty-five, happy at work, ambitious and hopeful.

◆

The difficult part was persuading people to deposit money with BTF. With so many Nissan Sunnys and Honda Civics and so many bright-looking, aggressive young men and women out on the streets pursuing money, there was hardly enough to go round. Yemisi led from the outset: it seemed as though when men saw her lovely thighs they just signed cheques for one hundred or two hundred thousand naira without thinking. In three months she had brought in five hundred thousand. Philip, through connections in his former bank, had brought in two million. I had brought in only a miserable one hundred and fifty thousand; fifty thousand was from my mother. We had to do it behind my father's back, for even with the new Nissan Sunny that picked me up from home for work and dropped me at the end of each day and my doubled salary, he was still sceptical about my new employer. The other hundred thousand came from an extremely wealthy uncle of my girlfriend, Robo, for whom depositing such a sum with my company was like fetching a teaspoon of salt water from an ocean. Even Amina had done almost as well as me: she'd persuaded some man to deposit one hundred thousand.

Philip had hinted to me at the beginning that since we were friends and I had the most banking experience in Treasury and Marketing, I should regard myself as the top person in the group.

But he soon began to sing a different tune at the endless pep talks: 'There is only one criterion for conferring seniority in this company, and that is performance, and performance means only one thing: how much money you bring into the company. It's that simple.' Yemisi had been paid bonuses for two months for her impressive performance, and Philip had taken her out to lunch; she was inevitably beginning to develop airs. I envied her wicked figure, and sometimes after walking all over Broad Street and The Marina and failing to prise even ten thousand naira out of anyone, and knowing I had to endure the disappointment in Philip's fanatical eyes when I reported yet again that I had not got any new deposits, I almost began to miss the peaceful stagnation of CDB.

Then I ran into Fati in the UTC cafeteria where I had gone for lunch after another series of fruitless meetings with people on my dwindling list of potential customers. Fati had entered the economics department at my university two years before I did, but was still there in my final year. For her, school had been a part-time thing; her main occupation was travelling around Europe and America to spend time with sundry boyfriends and keep her wardrobe current. Six feet tall, with a body honed by religious aerobics to athletic perfection and big flirtatious eyes, Fati was rumoured to be directly responsible for deadly quarrels between once best friends at the highest levels of government and commerce. When she did find time for the university, she had always turned to me for help with her schoolwork. And while we studied together she had sometimes been kind enough to have sex with me. It wasn't stated expressly, but I got the feeling that the sex was strictly in payment for helping her with her books. Since our graduation I had not heard from her.

When she saw me at UTC, she rose from her seat and enveloped me in an embrace reeking of perfume. Over lunch we caught up on what had happened in the preceding three years, and I told her of my frustrating struggle to get people to deposit money with BTF.

'I know a number of people who are worth approaching,' she said. 'One in particular, I think, is very promising. He's a businessman and he fronts for some very high-up people in government. He has tons of money and not much grey matter. He's doing everything possible to sleep with me, but it is out of the question as he is a really disgusting creature. I think I might be able to convince him to deposit some money with you.'

She gave me the phone number and address of her office (she ran her own interior decorating business) and of the flat in Surulere which she said she temporarily shared with a friend. I asked if we could spend some time together soon, go out somewhere for dinner, go to a nightclub, watch a video at my place, that sort of thing; try to relive old times. She smiled a deeply ambiguous smile and said she thought it best that we concentrate first on getting me some customers.

A week later Fati walked into the Treasury and Marketing Department office at BTF with one of the strangest human beings I've seen in my entire life. The fellow had a large forehead furrowed by lines of intense concentration as though everything around him was beyond his comprehension. His eyes were as small as peas. Thick tufts of hair grew out of his nose. His incisors were brownish yellow, and his teeth got even murkier in colour after the canines; when he opened his mouth, a rank gale, the odour of rotten eggs, blew across the room. He had a rattling laugh, like a motorcycle in bad repair, and his small eyes darted about with a look of alertness and cunning that made me think of a rat. He chafed at the boldly striped red and black three-piece suit which someone had put on his short thickset body. He had already loosened the two top buttons of the vest and the top button of his shirt, and the knot of the tie, which was the size of a football, lay on his chest. The way he kept pulling at and straining against his clothes I wouldn't have been surprised if he had taken them all off right there and then. Fati, noticing the amazement in my eyes, shrugged her shoulders as if to say: I told you he was disgusting. She had called earlier to say she was bringing the potential customer she had mentioned in UTC over to my office, and for me to be ready to talk him into depositing some money. She had assured me again that it shouldn't be too difficult as he wasn't the cleverest person alive. She said his name was Sawa.

Sawa said our office was very, very nice several times, accompanying his compliments with his rattling laugh, his little eyes swishing around the room as he spoke. I noticed that the eyes settled lustfully for a long while on Amina and Yemisi, who were on their desks pretending to be busy while peeping as often as they could at what appeared to be a gorilla in a half-undone three-piece circus suit.

'Obi is the classmate and good friend I mentioned to you,' Fati said to Sawa.

He covered my hand in a firm, hairy grip.

'I don't do business with finance house,' he said, 'but Fati inform me that your operations have high integrity and efficiency, and you are trustworthy to the highest.'

It sounded like a joke, like something taken from the innumerable Nigerian radio and television comedies which live off grammatical irregularities, but Sawa was in earnest. He spoke words like 'operations' and 'integrity' with special pride, as a mark of learning.

I thanked Fati for the recommendation and went on to explain what finance houses did and the various areas in which BTF invested customers' deposits. Borrowing from the glossy brochure which Philip had prepared on the company's operations and from *The Economist* and CNN and from my own imagination, I wove the image of a dynamic investment octopus with arms in all the major financial centres of the globe. It was, even if I say so myself, a virtuoso performance. In fact I thought momentarily that I had overdone it, for Sawa's face was completely clouded with confusion when I had finished. Even though I had gone one slow step at a time, the wrinkles on his forehead stood as tall as cassava ridges. Then he looked at Fati as though she were his financial advisor, and she smiled at him, and he smiled and laughed his rattling laugh, and his eyes swished around the room again, lingering again on Yemisi and Amina.

'Very good,' he said finally, 'I have extreme interest in international financial business. I will test you with some amount first, then if I see excellent performance on your part, I will make more substantial deposit. I will initiate the trasaction with one million naira for duration of six months.'

I wasn't sure I'd heard him right: one million was nearly ten times all the money I'd brought in for three months. With an additional deposit of one million, I would overtake Yemisi. Only Philip would have brought in more. But I managed to muster enough composure to act as if scores of customers lined up first thing every morning to deposit one million naira and more with me.

I offered him an interest rate of thirty per cent per annum, simple interest, payable up front. In the bitter war to attract depositors many finance companies and some merchant banks were already offering up to fifty per cent up front, but I told him that the higher the interest rate offered, the more difficult it would be for the finance company to meet its obligations and that only desperate finance houses with very few customers offered such risky rates. He accepted the rate without argument: he seemed more concerned with ogling Yemisi and Amina than with getting a good return on the money he was depositing.

When would we get his cheque, I asked, battling to keep my nervousness under control.

'You are free to dispatch your messenger downstairs to my vehicle and inform my driver to bring one box from the boot compartment of the vehicle,' Sawa said. 'The vehicle is dark blue Mercedes, v-boot, with tinted glass. In the meantime, you can give instruction for immediate preparation of necessary documents.'

I buzzed for a messenger and relayed Sawa's instructions for his driver, then in less than two minutes I fed the terms of the deposit into forms in my p.c. and printed out three sets of documents. I scanned them quickly for errors, then I signed and took them to Philip to counter-sign. His eyes grew as large as watermelons when he read through the papers.

'One million, fantastic!' he said. 'That is great work, Obi. Do you think I should come and meet the customer?'

'Later, I'll arrange for a lunch date or something like that,' I replied.

'Yes, that's a better idea. This is fantastic! If you are free, we must go out for lunch tomorrow. I've been meaning that we should go out for a long time now, but meetings and all this paperwork keep getting in the way. You know how it is.'

I said that I knew how it was.

'Fantastic, great, wonderful work, Obi,' Philip called after me as I left the room.

Among the documents he had signed was an agreement and voucher to pay a brokerage fee of three per cent of the deposit, in cash, to the facilitator of the transaction. BTF had up till then not paid me more than one point five per cent as brokerage fee, but for a single deposit of one million I thought three per cent was reasonable. Philip apparently agreed.

I returned to my office with the papers just as Sawa's driver, accompanied by our messenger, was depositing a big brown leather bag on my desk. Sawa unlocked the bag and dramatically flung it open, revealing tightly packed bundles of twenty naira notes still in Central Bank wrappers.

'I prefer to deal in raw cash,' Sawa said, laughing. 'I carry them in one-one million to avoid hardship of too much counting.'

I quickly checked the bundles of money and then gave Sawa the terms of the deposit to sign. He pulled out a gold pen from his suit and drew a gigantic signature, full of flourishes. He beamed smiles of self-congratulation at Fati, myself and the BTF messenger like a man who had just indisputably proven his virility in the face of great odds. He said he had some more business to attend to that morning. Fati said she, too, had things to do, and I saw them to the blue Mercedes. Before he left the office, Sawa threw one last look of longing at Yemisi and Amina and gave a brand new twenty-naira note to our messenger, who had hung around in a corner of the office like a hungry puppy after seeing the bag full of money.

I ran back to the office, taking three stairs at a time. Yemisi and Amina were in an uproar at the astonishing events they had just witnessed.

'Beauty and the beast,' Amina said. 'How can she appear in public with that animal?'

'I wouldn't mind appearing in public with a man who carries millions of naira in his boot even if he looked like a donkey,' Yemisi said, 'but, God knows, I would never let him touch me.'

'I couldn't be seen in public with someone that looks like that even if he had all the money in the Central Bank,' Amina insisted. 'God forbid!'

From the many slips in her tireless story-telling, we knew that Amina had slept with quite a number of men of all ages, so many that she frequently mixed up their names and dates. I knew that not all of them could be so much better than Sawa, so I wondered how much of her vehemence had to do with true revulsion and how much had to do with hypocrisy. But I was too excited to indulge in any banter.

I counted out the brokerage fee of thirty thousand naira from the deposit of one million and stuffed the money in three big envelopes. I told Philip that I had to go out to make some marketing calls and would not be back before the office closed for the day. He told me not to forget our lunch date for the next day and to fix a date as soon as possible when we could have lunch with Sawa.

Seated at the back of one of the Nissan Sunnys, my three envelopes of money beside my feet, I went and gorged myself on sautéed prawns and diced chicken in ginger sauce at Jaws Chinese Restaurant. Then I went to the shops behind Mandilas and bought my first designer suit: a charcoal by Canali, and three shirts, three designer ties and a bottle of Azzarro. I bought two of the severe ties he favoured for my father and designer perfume for Robo and my mother. At Cash and Carry I found a Sony 60 watt cassette player for my younger sister, Nwaka, who had just got into university and had been moaning that her lack of musical equipment made her life miserable.

That evening I went to Fati's place in Surulere and caught her, dressed in a white T-shirt and black shorts and carrying an overnight bag, on her way out of the flat. I thanked her profusely and gave her an envelope containing five thousand naira, telling her that it was a tiny token of appreciation from the company. She said I shouldn't have bothered, that I was a wonderful and treasured friend, that had I already forgotten I was the one who made it possible for her to graduate from university, but she pushed the money into her bag all the same. I told her that I *really* wanted to spend time with her soon. She smiled her ambiguous smile and kissed my neck and promised she would work out something and call me soon. That promise, I remember with great sorrow, was never fulfilled, despite hundreds of phone calls to the flat and her office and a huge birthday cake and flowers delivered by a BTF driver.

I took Robo to dinner at Shangri-La that night. Looking down at the lights of Lagos from the leafy penthouse restaurant, I felt like a warrior-king surveying the defenceless city he would soon gobble up. I slipped a hundred naira to the weary BTF driver as he dropped me off at home just before midnight.

◆

I'd never pimped for anyone in my life, but from the way Sawa's eyes fastened longingly on to women's bodies, I knew that the way to his wallet was through his genitals, and I immediately set about winning more of his patronage by that route. I was friendly with two fairly good-looking girls in my neighbourhood at Yaba – Queen and Brenda – who seemed ready to sleep with anybody who had a good car and some money. I'd heard stories from friends who had enjoyed their sexual favours. They were so generous, they had jointly earned the name 'expressway'. If a guy left a bar and said he planned to stop over by expressway and see if his luck would shine that night, we all knew what he meant.

I went by their flat the day after Sawa had made his deposit, a Tuesday. I explained that I had a very important business client and I wanted to give him a good time that weekend. I would be counting on them to come out with us to dinner and to a nightclub on Friday night. They said they had nothing planned for Friday, but that I would have to confirm that the date still stood by Thursday so they could make alternative plans if it didn't. They sounded very businesslike, and I was impressed.

I called Sawa that night and told him I would like us to go out with two beautiful women that Friday, if he didn't have other plans.

'Even if I have critical business meeting, I will suspend it,'

Sawa said. 'I am extremely interested. I hope the girls are very co-operative.'

'They are my good friends, and they *are* co-operative. Eight p.m. then, Friday?'

'Yes, please, don't fail at all, please.'

When I got to the government guest house where Sawa stayed whenever he was in Lagos, because of his government connections, he was twittering with nervous excitement, trussed up in a black suit. I gently told him it was a casual outing and shirt and trousers would do. He took off the jacket and the tie and examined himself in the large mirror in the living room of the guest house.

'How am I looking?' he asked me. I told him he looked very nice and his face broke into a huge smile.

We went in his blue Mercedes; I drove. Sawa said he was scared of driving in the city, and he didn't want his driver around him at night who he was scared could plot to kill him. I wanted to tell him that more people were murdered in Lagos during the day than at night, but I decided that might spoil the evening for him. There was so much power in the car that I was a little surprised when I brushed the brakes with my foot and the Mercedes actually slowed down. I told Sawa he had a great car. The Mercedes 300 was nothing, he said, compared to the Mercedes 500 and the BMW 5-series which he kept in his house in Abuja.

He told me about his experiences with Lagos women; one had stolen ten thousand naira from him while he slept; another had drugged his drink and stolen the watch he'd bought for three hundred pounds in England and the sunglasses he'd bought for five hundred marks in Germany. Another had stolen a cheque from his cheque book and forged his signature and gone to the bank to cash fifty thousand naira, but he had phoned the bank just in time and had her arrested.

'They have reptile behaviour,' he said. 'This time I don't follow any woman in this Lagos with exception of a highly trustworthy good friend like you guarantee her total honesty.'

I assured him the women we were going out with had total honesty and a lot more. He laughed his rattling laugh.

Brenda in tight jeans and a skimpy v-necked top, and Queen, in a tight aquamarine mini, looked very sexy. I noticed that Sawa began to salivate as they came towards the car. Queen's skin was lighter than Brenda's – she probably used more effective bleaching creams – and I marked her out for Sawa: for most of my countrymen and women the lighter the skin, the greater the beauty.

'This is tremendous beauty like Queen Sheba,' Sawa gushed at the women as I made the introductions, 'and those dresses are New York design, I am sure.'

Brenda told him that he looked great himself, and I feared for a moment that Sawa would hit the ground under the force of the compliment. He swelled up like a balloon and caressed his light blue shirt and black trousers as though to make them look even nicer.

We talked about where to eat; the girls said they liked Double 4, and we headed for Ikoyi. The restaurant was somewhat crowded. A few of my friends waved and asked questions with their eyes: Sawa and Brenda and Queen were not the kind of people I usually went out with. I smiled at my friends and looked straight ahead.

We all ate and drank heartily. Sawa and the girls ordered side dishes, ice cream and bottles of wine, and I silently wondered if the money I had budgeted would do. Sawa talked about his business triumphs. He had just won a contract to supply a hundred tractors to the Federal Ministry of Agriculture; he would be paid three times what it cost him to bring in the tractors from Taiwan. Another contract to build hostel blocks for a university was almost sealed, and another to build army barracks was on the way. Ministers ate out of his hand, carried contract papers to his house and knelt down to plead with him to accept jobs other people would kill for.

'Wow!' Queen said. 'I'm sure you can reach almost all the big government people any time you want.'

'Not almost all,' Sawa corrected her. 'I can enter the office of *all* of them, including even the president.'

'Even the president?' Brenda asked, her eyes widening.

'Yes, I don't like disturbing him because he is a very busy man, but any time I need to see him I have his personal phone number here,' Sawa said, and he patted his back pocket to show us precisely where he kept that priceless phone number.

Sawa told of the many contracts he had won and all the money he had made and all the expensive hotels he had slept in on business trips to all corners of Europe and the Far East. The man's ego jumped all over the place like a long-caged antelope enjoying its first moments of freedom. The girls humoured him brilliantly. Their eyes grew at the descriptions of hotels with diamond taps and first class aeroplane cabins where you could drink as much champagne as your stomach could carry. I remarked to myself that a man who told stories of this sort had no right to complain when a woman drugged him and stole his money and sunglasses. By eleven, about five bottles of sweet wine down the road, Sawa was beginning to show signs of advancing drunkenness. His little eyes were reddening rapidly, his rattling laugh dominated the restaurant. We had gone from Lagos to Munich to Zurich to Taipei to Hong Kong and back to Lagos in an odyssey of big contracts and beautiful hotels and business meetings and the wild sparkle of irresponsible power. The girls, too, were laughing a bit too loudly and their rate of intake of wine was growing alarmingly. The waiters were giving our table special attention. They smelt Sawa's money, or maybe,

81

considering how loud he had become, they had overheard some of his stories.

By twelve, we were the only ones left in the restaurant. Sawa and the girls looked ready to continue till morning, and the waiters, gathered around us in a circle of absolute devotion, looked like they wouldn't have minded. But I didn't want to have to carry my companion to the car and I asked for the bill. Sawa grabbed it from the waiter's tray when it came. I insisted it was my treat: his red eyes turned on me furiously, and with his trunk heaving as though he were suddenly short of breath, he told me with drunken hostility that he was going to pay the bill whether I liked it or not. Since he seemed prepared to engage in physical combat over the matter, I surrendered. He pulled an overburdened wallet out of his pocket and emptied a bunch of new naira notes on to the table. He then asked Queen to help him sort out the amount on the bill and a good tip for the waiters from the heap. She obliged readily with a smile, and Sawa watched with a self-congratulatory smile.

Sawa and Queen became intertwined like Siamese twins as we left the restaurant, and I noted, with awe, that she didn't seem to notice his rotten-egg breath. Brenda clung to me and I put an arm around her. I knew that in their state going to a nightclub was out of the question so I drove to Sawa's place. In the back of the car Sawa and Queen were making very distracting slurping noises.

Sawa was so far gone I had to take the keys from his unsteady hand to unlock the door to the guest house. He and Queen made a beeline for his bedroom and I led Brenda to the other room, grateful I had an emergency condom in my wallet.

◆

In time I became one of Sawa's best friends and confidantes, and his pimp. He told me that most people who claimed to be his friends only wanted to take some of his money, including some who were wealthier than he was. The world was a bad place, and he had found out that it was very dangerous to trust people. For some reason that was not clear to me, he assumed I had nobler motives than other people.

Only six years before he had been a poor teacher in a rural secondary school (that's where he got his educated man's words from), and the limits of his ambition had been to win a transfer to a city school where he would earn a better living by giving extra lessons to the children of the wealthy and be promoted one day to school principal. Then a cousin in the army, who had been brought up by Sawa's parents and was really like a brother, was given a lucrative post in government. Since Sawa was the only other person in the family with a modicum of education, and the cousin-brother had long known that he was a trustworthy person, he suggested that Sawa should resign from his teaching job and become his front (or business representative, as Sawa put it).

The cousin-brother gave purchase orders to companies registered in Sawa's name, say, to supply in bulk a year's requirement of drugs for all the hospitals in a particular state. Sawa would arrange for half the quantity of drugs to be delivered and get the state's health officials to certify that the purchase order had been fulfilled by giving them bribes several times higher than their pathetic salaries. Then he would pursue payment for the order, bulldozing vouchers past all bureaucratic hurdles, spraying bribes like an irrigation pump. The money would be paid into one of Sawa's bank accounts, and he would pass on the cousin-brother's share in cash, or purchase foreign currency with it which he would pay into the cousin-brother's bank account in Zurich.

Sawa and his cousin-brother grew in daring over time. They sometimes didn't bother to supply anything at all, just paid handsomer bribes and got the papers signed to say that deliveries had been made. In only a year Sawa made more money than he had ever dreamt of. Gone were the burning afternoons of severe headaches and back pain spent hoeing his farm beside his house in the rural school to supplement his family's diet; the nights of hunger and bitterness while waiting for the monthly salary that was already eaten up by debts even before it was paid, and the cruel contempt in the eyes of his wife and children. Sawa reminded you of this suffering all the time. By suffering so much, he seemed to imply, he had earned the right to his wealth even if it came from cooked-up supply receipts and systematic theft from public coffers. Anyway, only our country's socialists, radicals and people like that still thought that robbing the government was any sort of crime. Government money was juicy fruit hanging on a tree that belonged to no one; only a fool would, when given an opportunity, not help himself.

Over the years he developed his own connections and no longer relied solely on the cousin-brother. He had the private phone numbers of all the people in lucrative government positions, and a great part of his life was now spent going from one state capital to another, keeping warm all his contacts with men of power and sniffing round for good deals. He attended the numerous launchings of biographies of government officials – syrupy fiction of abysmally low quality by nonentities about nonentities; their birthdays and their wives' birthdays; the ceremonies where they were conferred with traditional chieftaincy titles; the naming ceremonies of their children and of their brothers' children; and the weddings of their sons, daughters, nephews and nieces – and he donated generously everywhere. He took out full-page advertisements in the newspapers every few months to congratulate them on their dynamism and their miraculous achievements in office and to assure them that the machinations of their enemies would come to naught. He retained informants near the highest points of government who alerted him when an official was about to fall so that he knew when not to attend a launching ceremony and when malaria would conveniently afflict him a day or two before a wedding. Sawa was a generous man, but men of power, he said, were almost always bastards so when they were ascendant you took all the shit they gave you in order to get what you wanted, but the moment they began to fall you got out of the way so they would have the hard, painful fall they richly deserved. But sometimes they defied all predictions and did not fall, or they fell and rose again, and you had to take ten times as much shit as you had before, to get close again to the tree hanging heavy with fruit. It was a life riddled with more uncertainties than astrology, and Sawa developed hypertension along the way.

A bit of his wealth began to flow in my direction. In addition to brokerage fees and bonuses on the deposits he made with BTF – a total of four million naira before the bubble burst – I earned commissions by acting as agent for the sale of a house in Ikoyi, which one of his friends in government had bought from the government at one-hundredth of the market value, and by helping to find buyers for a consignment of second-hand delivery vans which he and his cousin-brother had imported from Germany.

Early in 1992, Philip, whose driven eyes nearly shed tears of joy each time I scored another victory for BTF, made me manager of Treasury and Marketing, doubled my salary and permanently assigned one driver and one Nissan Sunny to me. He had a small office carved out for me next to his. Yemisi and Amina took my elevation in good grace and I bought them lunch almost daily in an eating place near our office of dubious sanitation and dangerously peppery fare, called *Executive Buka*, which was heavily patronised by the banking-finance company tribe. We nicknamed Sawa *gorilla millionaire*.

I acquired more designer suits and blazers, more shoes, more fragrances. I overhauled my father's nearly moribund Peugeot 504, replaced the ten-year-old rug in our living room and the exhausted upholstered easy chairs. I bought a microwave oven for my mother and a new radio for my father. I spoiled Nwaka with new clothes and chocolates and ice cream. I spoiled Robo, too, and she didn't grumble too loudly when I said I had to take Sawa out. I swore to her that I never slept with any of the women we went out with; they were too low class for me, I said.

My father's scepticism about my job changed to apprehension. In March 1992, he summoned my mother and me to a meeting in his study, lined with Ovid and Homer, Shakespeare and Marlowe. He called meetings in that study only on very grave matters and my mother and I arrived wearing appropriate looks of mourning.

'Obiora,' he began (he called my name in full only on very serious occasions), looking subdued and afraid behind his glasses, looking like he had suddenly shrunk in size, 'we are very, very happy with your success at work.'

He paused, my mother nodded vigorously; I waited for him to continue.

'But, we have brought you up in a humble Christian family and we have a duty to make sure that you live a fully Christian life. Like I said, we are very happy with your success at work and we are grateful to God for everything. All I want to say is that you should be very careful in everything you do. This country is a place of many temptations, and when you are young you want very many things, and you want all of them immediately. Sometimes you do not care how they come; you just want them. That is the road to doom and that is the road we want you to avoid. Easy money is very sweet, but it is also very dangerous. Don't get me wrong – I am not saying you have done anything wrong, we just want you to be very careful about who you deal with and in everything you do.'

'Daddy, I thank you for your advice and for your concern,' I said like an obedient son, feeling sorry for the old man. 'I'm not doing anything wrong; I've just been a bit lucky.'

He nodded sagely, then he went round and round in slow and aimless circles of advice like a man who had completely lost his way in a strange town. For people like my father, sudden wealth was inherently evil; it upset the order of the world – twenty-six-year-old sons became breadwinners, made more money in a week than their parents who had worked for thirty years made in a year and wore colognes that cost more money than the family's annual food bill. It was as though, in less than a year, I had supplanted him as the head of his house, as though I had married his wife and become the father of his children.

After what seemed like an eternity of directionless counselling, my father said, 'Let us pray.'

He fetched his huge old Bible from a drawer and read from the Book of Psalms. Then he knelt down and entrusted my future in that land of temptation and wickedness to the Heavenly Father. When he was through my mother led us in singing a song of praise to the Lord:

> His promises never fail
> His promises never fail
> Oh yes, the promises of my Father
> Will never ever fail.

Three months later I took a well-deserved three-week vacation and went with Robo to London. Bronzo, my friend from university, who came to pick us up from Victoria Station, looked at my grey single-breasted Louis Raphael suit, my tie by Profilo and my black shoes by Gucci, and at Robo's lovely peach dress and he let out a yell.

'I thought I heard there was recession in Nigeria,' he said. 'Do you work in the fucking finance house, or do you own the bloody thing?'

Glass, Not Diamond

My rise to designer-suit-wearing manager at BTF took about a year and a half; my fall to joblessness and pennilessness took only nine months, but those nine months, of stomach-churning anxiety and fear, felt like a hundred years. And even now I sometimes still have nightmares about that horrible sinking, and wake up with the psychosomatic ailments of that period: dull, lingering headaches, sudden diarrhoea, vicious tightness in the chest, constriction of the throat, acute insomnia.

It started, as most things start in Nigeria, in the form of rumours that gather strength and mutate as they swirl around: this or that finance company was having problems paying interest on deposits, this or that bank was quietly laying off workers. Stories appeared in the papers early in 1993 about finance companies which had defaulted on paying the insane interest rates they had offered to their depositors in the desperate scramble for money. Some of these depositors were themselves banks and finance companies and default in one financial institution badly wounded a number of others. In February Yemisi, who had mysterious but impeccable sources of information, told me that BTF had lost a lot of money in one of the finance companies that had crashed noisily the month before; it was called Kilimanjaro Finance. I felt like I had been immersed in a tub full of ice and water. The money I'd thought was safe in stock exchanges in London and New York (as BTF's promotional brochure claimed) was right there in Lagos, in places with disheartening names like Kilimanjaro Finance.

A week later Philip sacked Amina for low productivity. Apparently, supplying him and one of the members of the board of directors with sex regularly was, in the suddenly inclement business climate, no longer good enough reason to pay her a treasury officer's salary. Amina came by my office on her way out, red- and puffy-eyed, lugging a bag full of her gossip magazines. The tear marks on her face had cut swathes through heavy layers of rouge and smudged her thickly stacked red lipstick, making her look rather ridiculous.

'God will pay him back,' Amina said, her voice weak and bitter. 'I tried to talk to him, and he told his secretary to tell me he was busy. After all the work I've done here.'

'I'm sure you'll find something better,' I said.

'By the grace of God, I'll get a job a hundred times better than this wretched place,' she said, without conviction. 'I know you had nothing to do with it.'

I nodded in confirmation. I was manager only in name; Philip decided everything and had never thought it necessary even to mention his decisions to me.

'I know you will not do such a wicked thing to anybody,' she said. It sounded like a question.

'Take care of yourself,' I said, 'and do try to keep in touch.'

'God will punish him,' she said. Then she rested her big bag of gossip magazines on the floor, looked down for a short while, wiped her eyes, then she picked up the bag and left my office, sniffing as she went.

As she walked towards the staircase, carrying her big bag like a sack of stones, fear fell on the office as swiftly as death. From that day onwards we lived at the mercy of fearsome rumours about the state of BTF's finances. We, who had once spent hours confidently holding forth on the Nasdaq index and the price behaviour of Brent crude and about kpis and csfs, now spoke only in whispers. When I tried to make brave jokes about our situation, people smiled painfully, as though they had terrible sores in their mouths. Soon my courageous sense of humour atrophied.

A few weeks after Amina's departure, Philip sacked everyone in Operations, all the drivers except his own, one secretary and one messenger, and put the rest of us on half-salary. That was when my headaches began and the queasiness in my stomach along with acute insomnia. I worried about Sawa's deposit with us – how did you walk up to a man and tell him that the four million naira he had entrusted to you had gone up in smoke? Sawa was away in Europe on business and I awaited his return with great trepidation. I worried about my future. I had quickly become used to the affluent lifestyle of a financial industry executive: my wardrobe was filled with designer clothes, my dresser at home was like the display case in a perfume shop, but I had no savings. Almost all the money I'd made had gone into looking the part of a finance company manager. When I walked down the street in any one of my suits, the envious, oppressed eyes of lesser men followed me slavishly. When my Nissan Sunny went past a crowded busstop, the poor souls waiting for smoking *molues* stared at me as though, if they stared long enough, my status, my good fortune would somehow rub off on them. All that awe and envy I had come to regard as my entitlement, like rents payable to a feudal lord. How now did you begin to climb down from that height? Robo put her arm around my neck at a drinking joint in Obalende one night in March 1993, when I was as low as the bottom of a riverbed, pulled me close to her, and said: 'It's going to be all right, I'm sure.' I took her hand off angrily. I didn't want pity, even of the affectionate kind. I remember thinking at the time that when people begin to tell you that it's going to be all right in a solemn, pitying tone of voice, it usually means that your situation seems absolutely hopeless. Several evenings while watching TV at home with my parents I caught their eyes examining my face closely, as though they were scared I would kill myself.

There was virtually nothing to do at work: no one was depositing money with finance companies any more so there was no need to try to find new deposits, and we just hung around staring at each other or into space. The uncertainty became more and more unbearable and nearly every day I tried to build up enough courage to approach Philip and ask him exactly how badly we had been hit by the crisis. But whenever I went near his office all the courage I had stored up flowed away. Perhaps it was because I was too frightened of what his answer would be: it was better not to know, to continue to hope that things were not too bad or would somehow get better.

Philip's big confident shoulders shrank rapidly like low quality fabric. His eyes which once blazed with ambition seemed to have something peppery in them that often made him blink in pain. He became very taciturn, no more pep talks about being competitive, aggressive and so on. He got to work earlier than usual and locked himself in his office all day. Since he didn't come out even for lunch, I sometimes wondered if he'd stopped eating altogether.

He continued his savage cost-cutting, subletting half of BTF's office space to a company that marketed cable satellites, thus reducing BTF's spacious suite of offices to just his own office, mine and a general office as narrow as a pencil, where Yemisi, who had lost so much weight she looked like a street urchin, and had started leaving early every evening to attend prayer meetings, revivals and crusades, the sole surviving secretary,

Mrs Ofulue, and the sole surviving messenger, Kingsley, sat on desks arranged in a straight line, staring at the door. Philip quietly sold the desks, carpets, p.c.s, air conditioners and bits of partitioning which were left over from leasing out half the office space, and two of the Nissan Sunnys – leaving only his car and mine.

His strategy for dealing with customers was to admit to them that we were, like all other financial institutions, experiencing cash flow problems. It would anyway have been impossible to conceal that fact with our office cut to half its size and our staff strength even more drastically reduced in less than four months. He urged them to roll over their deposits with us, promising to pay them interest promptly. With the money saved from his cost-cutting, we had enough to make interest payments on time. Our customers meekly agreed to roll over. They'd heard that many other finance companies couldn't even pay interest – offices had become battlegrounds between groups of creditors who were scrambling to seize office cars and air conditioners, even office curtains – and they were grateful that our situation was not that bad. The upbeat early days of BTF were gone for good, but we appeared capable of limping along for a good while.

◆

Then one morning in the last week of May, I got to the office at ten a.m. (punctuality was no longer a priority) and found Sawa standing in the narrow general office, smouldering like nitric acid. Kingsley, the messenger, was the only one already at work.

'I reach here since eight o'clock,' Sawa said before I could say a word to him. 'I stand outside for more than one hour before your messenger come and open the door. I think you people have too much money now you don't care about your customers again.'

That obnoxious man, whose little eyes bulged with anger, whose forehead was ridged with distrust, whose neck was stiff with bitterness, was a totally different being from the easygoing Sawa I knew.

'I'm very sorry,' I said when I had got over the shock of seeing him there and so hostile. 'I had a few business calls to make this morning. How was your trip? I didn't think you would be away for so long. How long was it? Three months, I think. Or even more?'

Sawa had no interest in discussing his trip to Europe and said, 'I want to close my account. I need the money very urgent.'

When your deepest horror climbs to the surface and stares you in the face, you virtually need to learn a new language. After Sawa had declared that he wanted all his money back, four million naira all told, and I remembered how Philip had scrimped to pay amounts as low as fifty thousand as interest to smaller depositors, I suffered a terrible constriction in my throat. In that instant I knew how it felt to be a visitor in a strange country, nearly dead from frustration because you don't know enough of the local language to say even a thousandth of the things you need to say. That, I believe, was when a tightness in my chest and a tendency to speak too slowly or too quickly or not at all joined the list of psychosomatic illnesses I had to contend with.

'Let's go into my office,' was all I came out with after a long while.

'We have had some problems,' I said tentatively when we were seated. 'You know, there is a crisis in the financial industry, and a lot of our funds are trapped.'

'All that one doesn't concern me,' Sawa said. 'I have important thing to do with my money and I need it immediately.'

Though a great number of things were said, we didn't move beyond that basic position: Sawa wanted all his money immediately versus BTF couldn't pay him his money, at least not immediately (or in the foreseeable future).

'Let's wait for my MD to come in,' I said at length. 'I think we need to discuss this with him.'

But Sawa reacted with hostility even to that unavoidable proposal. 'I don't like your delaying method,' he said. 'I hand all the money over to you directly, and I need direct reply from you.'

'But you are an international businessman; you know how companies work,' I pleaded. 'My MD takes all the important decisions, and he needs to be here so we can work out a solution to the matter together.'

'The only solution,' Sawa said, 'is you pay me my money now.'

Mercifully, Philip came in within twenty minutes. I'd told Kingsley to let me know as soon as he arrived. Without giving Philip any warning, I took Sawa to his office. As we walked in Philip's face quickly tried on a number of expressions then settled for an insipid, false cheerfulness.

'Chief Sawa, long time,' he said, rising to his feet, a poor smile on his face. 'After a while we thought you had decided to settle in Amsterdam or Zurich. The way this country is going no one would have blamed you. It's really nice to see you.'

Sawa sat down without a word, ignoring Philip's outstretched hand. I sat beside Sawa. Philip seated himself again, his insipid smile gone. Sawa looked at me, I looked back at him. He kept his eyes on me so I leaned forward, cleared my throat and broke the bad news to Philip.

It took Philip a while to take it in. He evidently suffered that terrible constriction of the throat I had experienced earlier. He started to speak, but only a blabbery sound came out, like baby-talk, and he kept quiet.

'Chief,' he said finally, 'as Obi must have explained to you,

94

these are difficult times for the financial industry. Nevertheless, you are a priority customer, you have helped us a lot and we don't want to cause you any inconvenience. I'd like you to give me a week to run around and see how much money I can put together. There are a number of payments we are expecting and everything that comes in will be kept for you.'

'You think I'm a small boy?' Sawa said, his voice rising, his chest heaving. 'You think you can tell me all those trick stories and I will believe you? You think I haven't heard what you and your brother finance house are doing to people? Please I need my money now-now, I have important things to do.'

'Chief, please, I appeal to you to exercise some patience,' Philip said. 'It's a bad time for everybody, but we will do our best to get you a substantial sum of money in the next few days.'

'I think you people are playing with me!' Sawa shouted, leaping to his feet. 'You don't know me, that's why you are behaving like this! If you know me well, you won't try to play any game with me!'

'It's not a game, Chief,' I said, also getting up. 'Please calm down.'

'Are you giving me my money now, or do you want me to show you what I can do?' Sawa asked, now burning like gasoline.

'I appeal to you to please calm down,' Philip said.

'Don't appeal to me! I don't want to calm down!' Sawa shouted, showering saliva-pellets into Philips face. 'Are you giving me my money, or do you want to see my true colour?'

Philip was in the middle of another forlorn appeal when Sawa got up and stalked out of the office. 'You will know me today,' he promised as he banged the door.

I turned to Philip. He looked like the weariest man in the world. I noted the rough stunted quills of beard on his normally clean-shaven face, the careless contours of his usually impeccable designer shirt, the painful fluttering of his eyelids as though Sawa had thrown a fistful of pepper into his eyes.

'What are we going to do?' I asked, feeling uncomfortable at asking such a heavy question of such an overloaded man.

'I'll think of something,' he said. 'You may return to your office. If I need you, I'll let you know.'

Sawa returned an hour later with five policemen, all armed with automatic rifles. One of them barged into my office and ordered me to follow him. I did, and he led the way to Philip's office where Philip, standing behind his desk, was flanked by two more. Sawa stood in a corner of the room shouting dementedly.

'. . . I give them excellent treatment! Like my own brothers! In fact the good treatment I give these people I cannot give to my own family! They know all my secret, I swear to God! I trust them more than I trust anybody! Not knowing that the plan they have is fraudulent plan! They bring me nearer to them so that they can finish me off totally! And I follow them like a fool! In fact they are very dangerous to the society!'

The policemen all nodded, agreeing with Sawa, as though merely from looking at Philip and me they could see we were exactly the kind of backstabbing crooks Sawa was describing.

'Please, Chief Sawa – ' Philip began.

'Don't call my name!' Sawa spluttered. 'I don't like criminal elements calling my name anyhow. Are you ready to pay me my money, or do we go down to the station?'

'I think we should go to the station; no need to waste time,' one of the policemen said. He had sergeant's stripes and a vicious coppery face mottled with patches of a dark skin disease.

'I am not a wicked person,' Sawa said. 'They wanted to kill me, still yet I am not a wicked person to them. If they can pay me my money here, I will forget everything. All I want is my money, not to punish them. Are you going to give me my money here, or do you want to pay at the station?'

Yemisi and Mrs Ofulue had come in by then and they and Kingsley stood by the door watching. The room stank of stale police sweat and the rotten-egg winds that blew out of Sawa's mouth. The policemen fiddled with their rifles, yawned at the time-wasting talk, glared at Philip and me.

'I have offered you one million,' Philip said to Sawa. 'Even that money is borrowed money. Please take it for now and – '

'Is it one million I deposit with you?' Sawa asked, walking up to where Philip stood and directing the force of his breath right into Philip's face. 'You want to pay me in pieces so the money will be useless to me, not so? You think I don't know all your tricks? You think you are very clever?'

'Sergeant, please help me to beg him to – ' Philip began, but Sawa cut him short.

'Did the sergeant deposit money with you? Is it you and the sergeant that have been doing business? You want to involve him now, not so? Did the sergeant spend my money with you?'

'No,' the sergeant said quickly, as though he was afraid Philip would somehow rope him in. 'Chief, I think you are too soft with these people,' the skin-diseased sergeant added. 'Let's go to the station. I think we can change their minds there.'

The other policemen supported the suggestion enthusiastically. Mrs Ofulue pleaded with them to have mercy. The police station was not a solution, she said, it would only make matters worse. Sawa turned on her: 'You want him to eat my money and go free, right? You are part of the plan, not so? Will you pay the money for him? Do you want to go to the station for him?'

Mrs Ofulue moved back a few steps. Sawa turned to the policemen. 'Bring them,' he said, pointing to Philip and me.

The goons grabbed each of Philip's arms and jerked him forward, even though he had not (and could not) put up any resistance. Philip's eyes became distant, disinterested. His soul seemed to have sought refuge in a saner place, leaving only an insensible physical husk. One of the policemen grabbed my shoulder and shoved me towards the door, and another unslung his rifle. I heard in my mind the horrible crack of thumbnails, perceived the odour of burning flesh, felt the heavy thuds of a rifle butt against my rib cage. Suddenly Yemisi began to cry like one of those Lagos rains that start reluctantly, almost noiselessly, and quickly explode into a storm of clashing cymbals and drum rolls. Mrs Ofulue joined in with a plaintive soprano. Yemisi grabbed Philip's waist and planted her head against his chest, making it clear that if they were going to drag Philip away they would have to take her with them. Mrs Ofulue again followed Yemisi's lead and covered me with her substantial body; her smell of Vaseline Intensive Care lotion filled my nostrils and drops of her emergency tears fell on my left ear.

The policemen, while still holding Philip, turned to Sawa for directions.

'Obstruction of arrest,' the sergeant muttered.

The injustice of the entire thing nearly brought tears to Sawa's eyes.

'Do they want me to leave my money and go?' he asked desolately. 'Do they think you pick four million naira from the ground? They want to destroy me, not so? I don't have the right to get my money again, not so?'

But despite all his protests about the cruel things Philip and I had done to him, Sawa couldn't bring himself to ask the police to rough-handle women. He decided on a tactical withdrawal.

'I am coming back exactly one week time to collect my money. If I hear story in one week time, you will see what I will do to you. That time if you like go and bring your mother and your whole village to come and cry for you. After they finish crying, you will pay me my money.'

Being a prudent businessman, Sawa snatched Philip's cheque

for one million which he had angrily rejected earlier and put it into his pocket.

◆

Though none of our other customers invaded the office with a group of armed men, we saw some other examples of derangement over the next few days, as depositors, driven insane by rumours that owners of distressed banks and finance companies were fleeing the country, came to BTF to demand instant repayment of their deposits, including some who had agreed to roll over only a few weeks before. When she was told BTF couldn't return her money, one old woman who did small government contracts and had had a deposit of three hundred thousand, took off her clothes, leaving on only a grimy slip and a half-empty, tattered bra, and wailed loudly: 'Which medicine man has done this to me? Were you sleeping, my Lord Jesus Christ? Where were you, my Lord, when my enemies conspired to destroy me?' Philip's uncle, who'd deposited a hundred thousand, collapsed on a seat, muttering: 'Only your blood can do this to you; it is the enemy inside you must fear, that is the real enemy.' Then he buried his head in his arms and deteriorated into incomprehensibility. Another customer, a burly beer trader, laughed out aloud and simply refused to accept that his money (five hundred thousand) might be gone forever: 'No, no, no, no, no, you people are joking. I am sure you are all joking, no, no, no, it's a big joke . . .' And we were, in fact, luckier than some others. In a merchant bank in Ikeja, after he'd been told there was no money to repay his deposit, a customer had gone home and returned with a machete. After chasing everyone out of the office, he had attacked everything in sight: desks, filing cabinets, p.c.s, TVs, until the police arrived and took him away. It was as though no expression of real grief was complete unless accompanied by hysteria, by craziness.

Every work day called forth new resources of crisis containment that we could not have imagined we possessed. We pleaded abjectly, we wrung our hands, we swore to God, we made promises and told lies freely, we offered instalmental repayment plans of increasing complexity, and whenever things got really hairy Yemisi's Lagos-rain weeping and Mrs Ofulue's accompanying soprano, like a pair of last-resort chemical weapons, spontaneously came to our rescue.

With only one day left of Sawa's one week ultimatum, I reminded Philip that our time was almost up. There was nothing to worry about, Philip said; he would handle Sawa. It was the most confident I'd seen him in a very long while, and I allowed myself to grow a little reed of hope: that maybe Philip would dip into those BTF investments which he had kept to himself so far and pay Sawa his money or at least a good part of it.

On the appointed day I came to the office early. Sawa called at eight a.m. to say he would be there by ten. By nine Philip was not yet around. I called his house, the phone kept ringing, no one answered. I figured he was out of his house and on his way to the office. But Philip was still not in by nine-fifteen, nor by nine-twenty, nor by nine-twenty-five. Panic seized hold of me by nine-forty. The last thing I wanted was to have to face Sawa and his armed policemen alone. Asking Yemisi to come along, I set out for Philip's place. Before we left I asked Mrs Ofulue to call Sawa and tell him that Philip had not come in and I had gone to search for him.

The sound of the doorbell travelled again and again all over Philip's house, a big two-storey building ringed by trees in the snug, upper-middle-class Alaka Estate, and returned to us empty-handed. An unthinkable thought, which I had refused to allow into my mind on the drive from the office, now took front seat –

100

that, like many other MDs of distressed finance companies and banks, Philip might have absconded.

I tried the door and it opened into the living room which was empty except for a few old yellowed newspapers and strips of twine. My heart shuddered like a light aeroplane encountering severe turbulence. Yemisi and I wandered around the house like lost sheep. We walked into the master bedroom where Philip had left behind an unopened packet of condoms on the floor and an old YSL T-shirt. In the bathroom empty cologne bottles and cans of shaving foam and bottles of shampoo and conditioning lotion were scattered all over the ceramic floor. In the kitchen there was a stack of dirty dishes in the brand new light blue sink and two empty bottles of Hennessey on the floor. Four tall plastic dustbins were piled high with old papers and more empty bottles and cans. Had he moved his things out gradually, or had he done it in one go, maybe the night before? I wondered. When had he started planning to go? Where had he gone to? England? The States? South America?

'What are we going to do?' Yemisi asked.

I didn't have any answers. The phone, which was lying in a corner of the living room, still had a dialling tone, and I called Mrs Ofulue and gave her the news in a flat voice. She began to gasp, as though she had suddenly become asthmatic, and I asked her to close up the office and to remain at home till I sent a message to her. I dropped Yemisi at her place and I went home.

◆

Sawa and his five armed policemen grabbed me from my house three days after Philip had fled, while I was still wondering when to get in touch with him and what to tell him. Fortunately my parents were at work and did not see me being pushed into the back of a new grey GM pick-up truck which bore the logo of

101

one of Sawa's companies. The sergeant with the skin-diseased face got into the cab with the driver, the others piled into the back with me, and we took off with Sawa's Mercedes trailing us. People, among whom I recognised a few faces from the neighbourhood, gaped at me from the surrounding streets, gaped with their mouths and noses wide open. We were soon out of the quiet streets around my house and in the full glare of the crowds on Murtala Muhammed Way, and the crawling, bad-tempered mid-morning traffic. While caught up in traffic, I had often seen people in the back of police vans; some I had observed laughing and chatting with their captors, waving their handcuffs about gaily; others had stared morosely into space, miserable and bitter. I lowered my head and examined the floor of the van, trying to hide my face without making it obvious. The ride to the police station at Alagbon stretched through several millennia.

It was my first visit to a police station. The scurrying about and whispering and the disorder and squalor around and inside the old unkempt colonial-era bungalow, the huddle of victims in various stages of misery and resignation and the horrible, pervasive smell of faeces and urine, suggested that this was not a place where wrongs were righted but one in which they were multiplied and then multiplied again. The inspector in charge of my case was called Philibus. He was a short man with a wide, tough muscular body like a tightly packed bag of yams. But his face was not tough at all; it broke easily into smiles – a face of genial corruption. When we got into the station, the sergeant in the lead, I and the other four behind him, with Sawa bringing up the rear, Philibus abruptly dismissed a small crowd of arguing and pleading supplicants standing in front of him and led us to his office off a filthy passage. He had a jerky walk as though an invisible person behind him prodded him in the back to move him on. He carried a sheaf of files rolled into a pipe under his left arm.

Sawa, in a huge, billowing mauve *babanriga*, launched into his usual tirade about how Philip and I had defrauded him.

'Now their plan is that the other one will run away and go and keep the money in their bank account abroad and after, this one, this thief, will go and get his share,' Sawa said. 'I made big mistake of being good to this people, I suppose to arrest them the other time, but I am just too kind.'

Philibus and the others commiserated with Sawa, cursed all the finance company thieves who had stolen hardworking people's money to buy new suits and flashy cars and promised him that everything would be done to teach me a lesson I'd never forget. But as soon as Sawa and his mighty *babanriga* disappeared from sight, the policemen began to abuse him in unison: 'Thief, bastard, greedy man, dirty mouth,' they called him, 'you steal our money with your army friends and go and put in finance house to make hundred per cent profit. You don't know that God is watching you, that He knows the bad things you did to get that money, that it is God that is punishing you now by making the money run away. Idiot, useless man, bastard, you come here to give us order with your dirty mouth smelling like gutter as if we are your houseboy.'

Philibus, beaming like a fluorescent bulb, then offered me a deal. Upon payment of a lump sum fee of ten thousand naira, I would be allowed to go home and thereafter report to the station five days a week, a few hours each day. In the meantime, he would give Sawa the impression that I was being held in the station. If I didn't have any money on me, he would send one of his people with me to collect it. If I declined the offer, he would regretfully have to put me in a cell which, as he put it, was 'not a good place at all'. I wasted no time in accepting the offer.

◆

We hung around the station all day, those MDs and managers of failed banks and finance companies who had not fled abroad, with murderers, armed robbers and con men. We watched Philibus come and go, tightly packed but highly mobile, cutting deals, smiling all day long, the roll of files always under his left arm. Some among us still clung to their designer suits and carried themselves with a full measure of corporate self-importance; others, like me, wore faded jeans, crumpled shirts and old sandals. Some made plans for the future, reminisced about old triumphs; I and many others listened wearily and said very little. Around the station the smells of various designer *eaux-de-toilette* combined with the police station's smell of old faeces and urine to produce a horribly repellent odour. It was as if two of the worst kinds of putrefaction in the nation had joined forces, which in a sense was true, for behind the veneer of fashionable suits and the spouting of fashionable finance industry words (like 'arbitraging', 'intermediation', etc.), our class of young and not-so-young bankers (and probably my entire generation of Nigerians) harboured a monstrous, vicious corruption and greed that matched and perhaps even exceeded the age old corruption of the police.

It is the kind of greed that builds nations, builds what mankind sometimes calls civilisations, and we all agreed, as we lolled about the station aimlessly, that we had possessed enough greed among us to transform our country, to make it nearly as 'civilised' as the wealthy nations of the world. But it was a greed that had turned inwards, like acid biting the walls of an empty stomach, because there had been too much greed prowling about and hardly any worthwhile controls. Unharnessed, that greed had gone berserk, had eaten up all the integrity in the financial system of which we'd lately been a part and earned us a multitude of enemies baying for our blood like wild dogs.

Sawa came to the station two or three times a week to make

sure I was still being kept in custody. Once I overheard Philibus telling him about the 'thorough investigations' being made into the case, the 'serious interrogation' I was undergoing. Sawa nodded his big head with satisfaction and his pea-like eyes lit up sadistically. It took a lot of effort to restrain myself from bursting into laughter.

Idejo, a plump, slow, unkempt fellow with a loud, raucous voice, was the most notorious member of our group. He had been MD of one of the flashiest finance companies, called something like Hibiscus or Jacaranda or Magnolia. All his marketing officers had been very light-skinned women, shapely and gorgeously dressed, and at one time he had employed ten of them. Before he fell he had been offering interest at ten per cent a month (BTF never went above sixty per cent per annum) and had accumulated deposits of more than two hundred million. The police had seized sixteen top of the range cars from his place – Mercedes Benzes, BMWs and Lexuses – and he boasted that the fleet at his London home was even more impressive. He had taken down with him more than twenty other finance companies and five merchant banks.

One day, about three weeks after Sawa had arrested me, Idejo, who was being vilified in the press as the Lucifer of the financial industry, the avaricious, ruthless, heartless destroyer of the Nigerian financial system, walked on to a plane at Murtala Muhammed International Airport and flew away into exile. The news came to us through an agitated man of about forty, with the stomach of a heavily pregnant woman, the MD of one of the hapless finance companies who had fallen victim to Idejo. This man came into the station, breathless, at nine a.m. to report to Philibus that he had heard from a friend that someone who looked like Idejo had boarded a Swissair flight the night before. In reply, Philibus told him that Idejo had not committed any crime and was free to go anywhere he wished like any other citizen.

'I will quote for you the exact section of the criminal code which says that any matter of business arrangement is a civil matter not a criminal offence,' Philibus said to the MD in an uncharacteristically harsh voice.

'But you told me you were holding his passport,' the poor man said. 'Don't you have a conscience? How can you talk to me like this after all the money you took from me?'

'Who did you give money to?' Philibus demanded fiercely. 'If you are not careful, I will arrest you for making false accusations. Go and ask people. I don't fear anybody.'

The executive walked out of the station with a painful limp as though the bad news had hit him in the leg like a bullet. About five of us had listened to this exchange, standing along the passage outside Philibus's office. A few minutes later the inspector strutted past us triumphantly, even more muscular than usual. His fellows near the counter, who had also eavesdropped, congratulated him with smiles.

'Foolish man,' Philibus said, 'imagine him coming here to tell lies against me, that he gave me money, coming here to show me nonsense second-hand coat and *ashawo* perfume. I did not want to disgrace him, but he was the one that brought the disgrace on himself. You give money to somebody, the person invest the money, the money is lost, what is the criminal offence there?'

'Don't mind them,' said one corporal, 'they are all tief.'

The policemen laughed with a lot of joy: they had triumphed over a member of the annoyingly affluent class who owned nice cars, suits and perfumes.

'Let him report me anywhere,' Philibus said. 'I can defend myself any time they call me. It is not a criminal offence.'

There were no stable categories in that world: legality and illegality mingled freely, as did cruelty and farce. If you paid a high enough bribe, a civil matter would become a criminal offence; if your victim paid a high enough bribe, the criminal offence would become, once again, a civil matter – like a seesaw.

After one more month, Sawa finally lost all interest in Philibus's circular burlesque of thorough investigations and serious interrogation. The police had handed over to him my official Nissan Sunny, which they'd seized from my house, and had let him carry away all the equipment in BTF's office. After that he no longer came to the station. Philibus offered 'to close my case file' for a fee of ten thousand naira. Having acquired some experience in police station culture during the preceding weeks, I counter-offered one thousand.

'I cannot believe you are arguing with me over money after everything I have done for you,' Philibus said, looking pained.

But it was all part of the ritual, and after we had haggled for a while and settled on four thousand, Philibus threw me one of his fluorescent bulb smiles.

'We don't pray for trouble in this world,' he said, 'but the country is too bad now, and if you have any police problem anywhere, come and look for me and I will see if I can assist.'

'I will always remember that,' I said.

◆

For a few months I suffered from the illusion that I could put my bone-splintering fall behind me and resume my interrupted life of upward mobility, though I accepted that it would probably have to be at a reduced speed. I called up colleagues who had not been claimed by the crash and asked them to let me know if they heard of any job openings. I dry cleaned my designer suits and drove into central Lagos on most working days, and though I no longer had a gleaming Nissan Sunny and had to make do with my father's Peugeot 504, I still thought I cut a fine figure.

At my first job interview I came upon a buzzing sea of young men in ageing undersized suits and young women in fallen-apart formal attire, penned into the cavernous auditorium of the Law School – more than six hundred of them – for an aptitude test of four parts. That was only the first step in a tortuous process to fill two entry level positions for university graduates in a merchant bank. I walked back to my car and drove away, saying to myself that to bring six hundred people together to compete for two jobs was heartless. A friend who worked for an American-owned management consulting firm said his firm couldn't hire me because I had a second class lower degree and the minimum they took was a second class upper, but that if I went to the University of Lagos and got an MBA, he would get me into the firm. Two more years back in school, lectures, exams and all that, for a job that would pay at most seven thousand naira a month (less than two hundred dollars at that time, less than ninety as I write in the autumn of 1995), about a tenth of what I had made in some good months in BTF. I didn't give the idea a second thought.

That offer of a job two years and an MBA away was, however, the only one I got. The already depressed state of the banks was worsened by a new military government – the third government we had in that unforgettable year – which, afflicted with economic illiteracy amongst many other serious illnesses, fixed the interest rate on deposits, by decree, at fifteen per cent. Inflation at the time, even by the extremely conservative estimates of the Central Bank, was above fifty per cent, and in a matter of days the government had succeeded in wiping out what little business was left to financial institutions. My mother, scared of my growing desperation, offered to lend me money to start a small business of my own, but I knew I wasn't cut out for tramping around Lagos begging for orders; buying and selling was even more horrifying. And so, like a cube of sugar, the illusion that I would soon be back on my feet dissolved.

By brutal coincidence, my father's civil service career of more than thirty years ended abruptly at about this time. The head of his ministry, freshly appointed by the latest government, had set up a panel of inquiry into a government company with a retired brigadier as chairman and my father as secretary. My father had been very impressed with the brigadier, had gushed about how trim he was, lean as an electric pole, one of the few soldiers around who looked like a soldier. The brigadier, my father said, woke up at five thirty every day and jogged five kilometres, was one of the finest squash players in the country, had a reputation for honesty, was a straightforward, humble man. With his many years of experience in the civil service, my father knew that the first thing you did when you were asked to be part of a panel of inquiry was to find out the kind of conclusion the person setting up the panel wanted, and then go ahead to reach that conclusion. But the brigadier who played squash better than anyone else in the country, who jogged five kilometres and was honest and straightforward and so on, affected my father's head like marijuana. Instead of checking to see what the minister wanted, my father began to talk of digging for the truth. Warnings were whispered to my father by two people planted on the panel to ensure it made the right findings, but the warnings could not penetrate his narcotic haze. Led by the brigadier, he went on to write a report in elevated prose which praised the managing director of the government company for transforming it from a subvention black hole into a profitable concern – perhaps the first person to do so with a government company anywhere in the country in more than twenty years. What my father had foolishly failed to realise was that it was precisely because the company had made profits that the panel was being set up: to find the managing director guilty of all the crimes in this world and the next, to get him out of the way, and put in someone who would be less interested in making profits and more concerned with seeing that the relevant pockets were stashed and stashed until they burst. Whenever my father told the story afterwards he would repeat that point over and over again: 'My crime was saying that an innocent man was innocent, that was my crime, that was why they threw me out,' until an old man from our hometown who had come to commiserate with him retorted angrily, 'Is there a little child in this country who does not know that a man is only innocent when those who hold power say he is innocent; if they say he is guilty, then every fool knows he is guilty. Is there any child who does not know that?'

My father's foolishness cost him dear. Three days after the report was submitted, the minister sent for him. From behind his wide, cluttered desk and gold-rimmed glasses, the little minister silently watched my father for what seemed like one hour. Sweat broke out on my father's body; the narcotic haze began to clear from his mind. He avoided the minister's chilly, dagger-point stare and examined the several rows of photographs of past ministers on the wall.

'Why did you allow tribal sentiments to stop you from doing your job properly?' the minister asked finally, pointing a disgusted finger at the panel's report which lay at the edge of the ministerial desk and had suddenly begun to look like damning evidence in a murder trial. The managing director of the government company praised in the report was, like my father, Igbo.

Before my father could respond the minister snapped: 'I have to attend a very important meeting right now so don't disturb me. Take your bundle of rubbish and get out,' and he shoved the report off the table and it landed with a muffled, ominous thud on the opulent rug.

Even after thirty years in the civil service, my father had not learnt true subservience. Instead of going flat on his belly to beg for mercy, which might have worked wonders, he picked up the report and left the office. He drove home, locked himself in his study and wrote a treatise of thirty pages, in the same elevated prose that had put him in trouble in the first place, essentially re-affirming that the panel had done its job properly. A stubborn man my father is in his own way, but in his treatise he left open a window of compromise by suggesting that perhaps additional facts might now be in the honourable minister's possession which would colour the matter differently. He did not forget to mention his thirty years and more of meritorious service, his wife and three children, his undying loyalty to the minister. The next morning my mother woke me and my sister, Nwaka, for special morning prayers in my father's study. He read from the book of Psalms and tremulously called upon the Lord to show His Face, to ensure that Truth was not defeated by Falsehood. My mother, as always, led us in singing a song of praise:

> I know my Lord is able
> Come rain, come shine
> Come joy, come sorrow
> I know my Lord is able

Fortified with prayer, psalm and song of praise, my father took his novella to the minister's office. The minister replied later that afternoon with a letter of ten lines compulsorily retiring my father from the civil service.

My father ran to the squash-playing brigadier, and the brigadier, terribly outraged, asked him to write yet another treatise, addressed this time to the head of state, the secretary to the federal government and other great personages, and said that he would personally carry these treatises to the persons concerned and also put in a firm word. This time my father covered fifty pages and had to insert a table of contents, and we prayed for two hours, read five psalms, sang three songs of praise. As I write these lines, twenty-three months later, my father has yet to receive any kind of reply.

Our house in Yaba was rented by the government, and the

minister, determined to grind his former underling to a pulp, sent a letter to our landlord, Adeyemo, notifying him that as of the date of that letter, the government was no longer interested in leasing the property. He further advised Adeyemo to eject immediately anyone currently occupying the house. Adeyemo had spent many evenings sympathising with my father, recounting how he was similarly hounded out of UAC, failing to mention that in his own case he had been unable to account for a lot of money and had been fortunate to get away with only summary dismissal. Anyway, because he was our family friend, we had no doubt that he would let my father lease the house privately at a moderate rent. But house rents were rising amazingly all over Lagos and the laws of economics proved more persuasive than a friendship of twenty years. An insurance company, Adeyemo said, had offered him two hundred thousand a year for the house and was going to pay him for five years in advance. If my father could match their offer and give him a cheque for one million in a week as the insurance company had promised to do, he would let us remain. One million! my father roared like a jet plane, one million! We had been thinking of a rent of fifty thousand a year and my father had said he would plead with Adeyemo to let him pay it in two instalments. There was no need to even try to appeal to him: to travel from fifty thousand to one million would have been for us more difficult than trying to get from Lagos to Los Angeles by bicycle.

We had taken that solid, airy two-storey house, our home for twenty years, for granted: four bedrooms and a study, a large living room with six tall windows, five toilets and four baths. And a small garden which received bursts of attention when, once in a while, either of my parents would lament at how the beautiful garden had gone to seed, get everyone to weed it, buy new plants and manure, excavate the watering hose, and spend the next three weeks, maximum a month, padding about every evening, exclaiming at how well the plants were doing, after which the garden would be forgotten again for six or seven months. Being a much doted-upon only son, I had been given the room on the ground floor in my first year at university and my parents had pretended not to notice when Robo, and occasional strays, spent the night. I learnt how to drive a car on the lawn outside, on the same lawn where our parents had given one birthday party a year for their three young children even though our birthdays were months apart.

A few days into 1994 we moved from the Yaba house to a three-bedroom flat in a block of six belonging to a distant relation of my father's in the outer reaches of Isolo. We had become part of an involuntary exodus that had been going on for years, of once middle-class families being carried by market forces from the central parts of Lagos and dumped on its edges like refuse. In those wastelands rushed into being by the city's insatiable hunger for new homes, sanitation and drainage are unknown, roads are dust-quarrying gullies in the dry season and treacherous swamps or angry floods when the rains come. The infernal noise from factory engines and the lung-corroding substances pumped out of their pistons together assault the misshapen blocks of flats which look like the mass-produced designs of the same overworked unimaginative draftsman. Though Lagos as a whole is ridden with armed robbers, Isolo has distinguished itself in this field, and within Isolo the new areas, into one of which we moved, are indisputably in first place. The clumps of bush that appear suddenly on the roadside, usually on parcels of land so far safe from frenetic construction because of ownership disputes, are excellent for ambush and the deep gullies on the roads assist robbers in bringing vehicles to a complete, helpless stop. Gunshots, angry voices, piercing wails tear your sleep to pieces nearly every night, fill you with terror.

From our new home my mother had to do a hellish drive to

her shop in Yaba every morning (leaving behind two disabled men – my father and me – brooding in the living room all day in front of the shiny black Sony Trinitron 21″ TV I bought when I was treasury manager in BTF) and another hellish drive back every evening through the most chaotic traffic in the whole of Lagos. Rushing home one day to catch one of the miserably acted and poorly translated soap operas from Mexico, immensely popular with a television audience that doesn't have too much to choose from, she drove into a deep gully in the middle of an Isolo street and broke the axle of her van which had given excellent service for ten years. She walked all the way home, about two miles, and was so completely covered in reddish brown dust when the entered the house that my father and I didn't recognise her for a moment. She stood in the living room, trembling with swallowed agony until my father led her to their room. That was when I noticed for the first time how much weight she had lost, how the struggle of the previous months had flattened her stomach and lopped off half of her nicely rounded backside.

My father seemed to have suffered a stroke. A big bone of impotence wedged itself in his throat and allowed him only fractured imitations of speech, and he stared into space, rheumy-eyed, for hours on end. During the family prayers which became even more frequent in our lives, my mother began to sound as if she was warning the Lord that her patience with Him was running out, 'We have waited for You to show us the way, we have waited oh Lord, we have *waited* . . .' in a bitter tone. But when my father prayed he sounded serene, as though he was past caring, was content to let the will of the Lord be done, however unfair it seemed. In that cramped, sorrowful flat, with window louvres that broke into pieces if you didn't shut them with great care, and toilet seats that came apart under you and turned into jagged weapons anxious to pierce your tenderest parts, depression began to choke me like smoke-plumes from a car's exhaust.

◆

When I was still a successful financial executive at BTF, I remember marvelling at the astonishing desperation of people trying to leave the country. I and many in the comfortable professional classes wondered, in our pseudo-Oxbridge, pseudo-Texan, pseudo-everywhere accents, why anyone would go to such lengths just to do menial jobs in Europe and America. When it was my turn to try to get away I discovered that the brain (and brawn) drain industry was far more extensive and inventive than we had ever imagined, and that the desperation seemed to be growing and spreading across all classes of our society by the minute.

Outside all the western embassies, long queues of visa applicants – managing directors of failed companies, frustrated senior civil servants, drug dealers masquerading as vicars, prostitutes claiming to be nuns, clutching enough genuine and bogus documents to fill several trailers – endured slashing rain and bitter sunshine. The rate of rejection was on the average ninety-five per cent, probably higher now. The rejected went home, bought new passports, changed from being vicars and nuns to being researchers attending academic conferences and officials of NGOs, and went back and rejoined the eternal queue. A resourceful Nigerian businessman opened an office in rural Transkei where Nigerians acquired South African nationality in thirty minutes and applied for visas as South Africans, cashing in on the continuing goodwill of Mandela's land.

Some went through Belize, some through Burkina Faso, others through Trinidad and Tobago; some crept across the Mexican border. Ships sailing from Lagos regularly discovered stowaways and it was rumoured that sadistic seamen had thrown many of them overboard. Sports teams melted away as soon as they cleared immigration, academics invited to conferences didn't even bother to deliver their papers before taking off to search for jobs as security guards or factory hands. Some shredded their Nigerian passports and flushed the pieces down airplane toilets, and arrived at Gatwick or Frankfurt or Amsterdam without nationality, stateless debris. One twenty-year-old boy entered Belgium illegally, married a fifty-year-old woman in order to become a Belgian (and European Union) citizen, and slit her throat when, in a moment of vanity, she showed him her small box of jewellery. He found out later that all the trinkets were made of glass, not diamonds, and then he slit his own throat.

For five months I developed and discarded intricate plans to get an American visa. Then I learnt through a friend who promoted musicians that a reggae band had been invited to perform at a musical festival outside New York. For fifty thousand naira they would add my name – as a keyboard player – to their visa applications, but I would have to attend an interview at the American embassy with the band.

Eleke Crescent, at five-thirty on the morning I went to the American embassy for my visa interview, was a place of ominous shadows. Well-dressed visa applicants, laden with papers, who had spent the night in the shacks by the lagoon near to the embassy in order to gain a good place in the endless visa queue, emerged in small groups from the semi-darkness like gangs of thieves. As the numbers grew rapidly and the queue twisted round and round the thick chains meant to maintain order of a kind, the improbability of getting a visa became more and more apparent. All the talk in the queue was about how heavily the odds were stacked against every applicant: many of the people near me had applied more than five times using different names, claiming widely different reasons for wanting to travel each time.

They had been refused on every occasion. In a couple of hours I became certain that mine was a hopeless quest.

To make matters worse, the members of the band I was supposed to be a part of kept glaring at me as we stood in the queue and rebuffed every attempt I made to be friendly: 'Hey, what sort of festival is it you guys are going for?' Silence. I tried again: 'I missed your concert at Laparius Gardens but a friend who went said it was wild.' Silence. Even if somehow the band was granted visas I was sure that the others would disown me when the time came. And I looked clearly out of place, the only one who didn't have greasy dreadlocks and marijuana-reddened eyes.

But the interview was surprisingly painless. The middle-aged Latina lady who interviewed us glanced at our passports and papers, asked a few simple questions, and then asked us to pick up our visas in a couple of days. It was over in ten minutes – so unbelievable that when I got my passport back, I kept opening it to check that the American visa was really there.

My parents could not bear the thought of their only son suffering in a strange land and they dug into their last reserves to give me one thousand US dollars in addition to buying my tickets. I had to go into America through New York's JFK airport with the band so that we would clear immigration as a group, and then on to Oakland alone. In spite of the huge expense, handling preparations for my trip re-infused my father with life. Whatever difficulties there were in America (and horror stories abounded, of Nigerian PhDs washing the corpses of the AIDS dead for a living, of random, mindless killings and so on), however tough things might be, he believed, like the thousands fleeing the country, that almost any place in the world had to be better than our rudderless nation.

The Surgeon and the Republican Party

I bought a car for fifteen hundred dollars at the end of January 1995, my sixth month in America. A 1982 Toyota Corolla, not too weathered, quite fast. One advantage of being on the grave-yard shift, not having any social life and living exclusively on junk food, was that you saved a good part of your wages. My first priority had been to get my own place, but the rains which began in late December and the bitterly cold nights had made waiting for buses very uncomfortable.

I bought a shelf-full of maps with my car, of Oakland and Berkeley, of Alameda County, of San Francisco, of the East Bay, of Northern California, and even a map of America showing all the fifty states and bits of Canada and Mexico. That was the extent of my sudden excitement, of the possibilities that danced about in my mind. But California's freeways and city streets, straightforward on the maps, had surprises in store for me. Junctions didn't appear where the maps seemed to say they would be; freeway numbers got jumbled up in my nervous brain, 980 became 880, 580 turned to 680. Impatient drivers chased me from the inside lanes to the outer lanes and back into the inside lanes. And every time I missed a car darting heedlessly into the freeway from a side street, or realised too late that I had just jumped a stop sign, or that I was going the wrong way down one of downtown Oakland's numerous one-way streets, I thought of my illegal status and what someone has described as the permanent state of war between American policemen and young black men. (I wasn't sure if the fact that I didn't have an African-American accent would make matters worse or better.)

Now I can look back and smile about those initiation rites, but in those days almost every drive within or outside Oakland demanded extraordinary mental labour.

I phoned Ego on the spur of the moment. I'd borne a grudge against her after the way she had treated me when I called her from the airport on my arrival in Oakland, but I had no friends to visit in my new car and even Ego was better than nothing. Besides, I said to myself, she might be able to introduce me to a woman. Ego, sounding guarded and suspicious at first, became very pleasant as soon as she confirmed that I wasn't planning to move into her house. 'Oh, you have to come over immediately,' she said, 'I've been thinking about you for months. I asked my mother last time I phoned Nigeria to find out from your parents where you were staying, but she hasn't called in a while, you know how rotten those Nigerian phones are. I've told my husband so much about you and we'd love to have you over for lunch,' and so on and so forth. I didn't want to appear desperate so I told her I was meeting friends for lunch that day but that I would call her again during the week so we could fix a date.

They lived in a gated community in affluent Blackhawk, more than twenty miles from Oakland. Though I had phoned Ego before I set off, and she'd said she would call the gate to let me in, the fat, shifty-eyed man at the security post still had to whisper something into the phone before allowing me past the immense gate. I felt like I was entering into a top secret military facility.

Identical sloping-roofed, stuccoed houses, surrounded by trees and gardens, all very neat and precise, lined both sides of the road. Ego's house was several rungs above those ones: on a hillside, a mighty stuccoed mansion set in the middle of splendid flower gardens, with a bean-shaped artificial lake beside the driveway and charming antique lampholders. Its roof of dark brown tiles sloped almost all the way to the ground. Ego rushed

119

out of the house as soon as I got out of my car and hugged me tightly.

'You've lost weight,' she said in a mother's rebuking tone, though she hadn't seen me for three years. 'It's so good to see you. How could you be in this place for so long without calling us? Don't you know you're the closest person to me in the whole of this country?'

I remembered her cold voice on the phone the day I had called her from Oakland airport the previous August, sharply telling me I wasn't welcome in her house, but I said nothing, just kept admiring the house. Ego looked very nice in a loose-fitting shirt and a pair of large khaki shorts and fetching strapless sandals; I noticed for the first time that she had straight, beautiful legs. Her skin was much lighter than I remembered it. I wondered if that was the product of toning creams or merely the sheen of wealth.

She put her left arm around me and led me into the house, cooing about how wonderful it was to have a brother so close by. She uncorked a bottle of champagne for me – Moët et Chandon – and set a plate full of grapes and crackers in front of me. Then she ran back to her fridge, skipping like a little girl, and brought me some chocolate cake and ice cream.

'You're in trouble today, Obi,' she said, when I told her I wouldn't be able to eat everything she was throwing my way. 'You will eat and eat and eat till your stomach bursts. If your stomach doesn't burst, I won't leave you alone!'

The large living room had severe modernist white and black upholstered chairs and side tables and shelves, accentuated by brilliant white walls. Too severe, I thought to myself, like something for display not for use, like a page from a glossy furniture catalogue blown up. Seeing as it must have cost a lot of money, I told her the furniture was very beautiful. She laughed and waved her arms about. I told her the house as a whole was very beautiful, without a doubt the most beautiful house I'd been into in my entire life. Again she went through the same laughing, waving routine. Compliments, I noticed, seriously disturbed her composure.

'My husband is performing surgery this morning; being married to a doctor is a tough life,' she said. But from the way she smiled, the way she glowed, I knew it was just talk. She didn't faintly look like someone having a tough life.

'He's always at work, always travelling for conferences,' she said.

I remarked that she had to find things to do to keep herself occupied in his absence.

'What I do is to watch soap operas and talk shows, and shop,' she said, and winked. 'In fact we're going shopping as soon as you've had your ice cream. I need to buy things for the house and a few clothes. I'll go and change now so we can leave once you are finished.'

And she skipped away. Through the window I saw a man who looked Asian watering his lawn in one of the identical houses below Ego's. I saw Mercedes Benzes, Acuras, Infinitis, Lexuses parked on driveways, open garage doors full of things, a man and his dog jogging gently beside the road. I was pleased with myself for knowing someone who lived in this community of the very comfortable, a countryman whose house dwarfed and looked down on the other affluent houses.

Ego came out half an hour later, wearing a jacket of intricate yellow and green patterns and a white T-shirt over brown slacks. Her eyes looked at her clothes and settled on mine, grovelling for compliments. I told her she looked absolutely lovely and she laughed and waved her arms about.

'There is only one other black family living here. The man is the Vice President of a big company in San Francisco, and there are two or three Indians and some Chinese and Koreans. Apart from that the rest are white,' Ego informed me proudly as we got into her bright red 1994 Honda Accord. 'We used to be part of Danville, the next town, but we are now a town of our own. We are about six thousand, the whole town, just six thousand. Can you imagine that?'

She laughed and waved her arms from side to side.

'If you work hard you can come and live in our community after a few years. You'll be the third black man to live here.' And she laughed again.

We bought groceries at a smart shopping centre, part of which was still under construction. I told her it was very impressive, she took the compliment as if she had built it herself. The groceries we bought filled the boot of the car.

'Now let's get some clothes, the real shopping,' she said with a mischievous smile.

It emerged, as we drove to the Stoneridge Mall, that life was not all a bed of roses for Ego. I asked her where she worked and a cloud passed over her glowing face.

'I stopped working more than six months ago, and I don't want to work again in this country,' she said angrily. 'As soon as I left the office people would start talking about me. Whenever I entered they would all stop talking and start watching me. As if I were a mad person. If you say something to someone, they would pretend not to have heard you. And I know they always heard everything I said. They just wanted to embarrass me. At a meeting one of them asked me where I was from. I said I was Nigerian and he said where the hell is that? He pretended he had never heard of Nigeria. Another one said it sounded like a place in Mexico, and they all started laughing.'

I fought hard and managed to stop myself from laughing out loud as I could see that for Ego it was no laughing matter. Nigerians, citizens of the largest black nation on earth, always found it difficult to accept that there are people living in this world who haven't heard of their big country. It is like being

122

told that you don't exist, and some have even resorted to fist fights in protest.

'Last week I went for a residents' meeting on our estate and immediately I entered, someone said something and they started laughing at me,' Ego went on angrily. 'I told my husband I would never go to any of those meetings again. If you ask someone a simple question they keep making you repeat yourself, as if they haven't heard you, when they have heard you perfectly. All I do now is sit at home and watch TV. I registered for a certificate course, but the lecturers spoke so fast I couldn't hear what they were saying so I stopped attending.'

She went on after a pause, 'My husband keeps saying that he's planning to go back to Nigeria to build a hospital and settle there, and just visit this place from time to time, but he keeps putting it off. I pray every day that we will go back soon.'

The interior of the Stoneridge mall cheered Ego up. It was awash with dazzling colours, filled with shoppers and gawkers and signs offering unbelievable deals, bulging with walking, jogging and office clothes, shoes and sunglasses and a hundred kinds of ice creams, chocolates and pizzas. I said it was beautiful, and she laughed and waved her arms about with that implied air of ownership. The mall reminded me of a story I'd heard from Ionesco, my Romanian former co-worker at the warehouses, about a Romanian woman, visiting her daughter in America after the overthrow of the Ceausescus, who burst into tears when she entered a shopping mall in New York. That magnificent symbol of capitalist consumerism, Ionesco said, had proved too much for the poor woman who had spent a large part of her life in bitter, sluggish queues for meat, milk and bread.

In Nordstrom, all the employees in the women's department seemed to know Ego well. They greeted us very warmly. I noticed that they knew of her aversion for people who spoke too fast and dragged every word they said to her, sounding as though they all had speech defects. Ego reciprocated with smiles, she laughed, waved her arms about, remembered each person's first name, even asked after their kids. One lady said it was proving impossible to pull her daughter away from the TV to do her homework. Ego remarked that there was an epidemic of that all over the world, and the women laughed long and hard at the joke. And Ego joined in: she knew this time that they weren't laughing at her; these were her friends, if only in a loose sense.

The pleasantries finally over, we got down to the serious business of buying clothes. Ego gathered from the display stands a pile of dresses, jackets and slacks taller than me. They all had exotic labels: Liz Claiborne Collection Saharienne, Maxou Printed Palazzo pants, Sigrid Olsen Verandah Collection, though they all looked ordinary enough to me. Then the process of selection began with me acting as judge. She would take an outfit, go to the fitting room and change into it, come back and model it for me, and then she would anxiously ask my opinion. Invariably I would say it was very nice, but that was never enough.

'What colour do you think it will go with?' she would ask, watching my face carefully as though to catch me out if I told a lie. 'Does it look too dull? Or too bright? Does it look too tight? Is it indecent? Or is it too loose, like a maternity gown? Is it good for evening wear? Or casual wear?' And on and on it went until I began to think that it would never end, that I would spend the rest of my life in Nordstrom trying to decide which neckline was too high or too low, which pair of slacks was too trendy or too old fashioned.

Salvation finally came my way when Ego looked at her watch and said she had to rush off because it was almost three o'clock and her husband would be back at four, and she had to get lunch ready. She gathered up the clothes that had passed her stringent tests – two trouser suits, two knitted tops, three slacks – and she added a bottle of Obsession on our way to the cash register. The cashier said it came to six hundred dollars odd, Ego pulled an American Express card out of her purse and slid it across the table, glancing at me with a triumphal smirk. I couldn't help remarking to myself that less than half of my countrymen earned six hundred dollars in a whole year. I was impressed with what I had seen.

We hurried back to her car so we would get to the house in time. She'd also wanted to go into Macy's, she said regretfully, but there was no time. America, I thought, might be full of people who spoke too fast and pretended not to know where Nigeria was, but it had huge department stores full of nice things. Ego wanted the nice things but not the stress of transplantation; a perfect world would be one in which she and her husband moved back to Lagos and Nordstrom and Macy's moved with them.

In forty minutes Ego filled the large dining table with dishes of fresh fish and chicken, trays of salads, rice and farina. Her husband, Ezendu, walked in, with perfect timing, as she was setting the table. He was a tall, enormous man with a strangely shaped head. It was in two parts: the northern region was vast and bare, not even a little wrinkle or a tiny pimple beneath his low-cut hair which was shiny with pomade, while the tapered southern part was crammed with a broad nose, a wide mouth, a bushy moustache.

'We were wondering where you had disappeared to,' he said to me, squeezing my hand. He was one of those people who test your manliness by trying to crush your bones in a handshake. I told him I'd been busy trying to settle down.

'It gets tougher every day,' he said. 'This country makes you a man. You can live in Nigeria all your life and live like a child, never be challenged once, but when you get to America, it begins to test you from the moment you step off the plane. It's a good thing; it toughens you up.'

I didn't agree with him that it was a good thing; I didn't think I needed any more toughening, but I held my peace.

We went together to the dining table. After the first mouthful Ezendu shouted compliments to his wife, who was still bringing in things from the kitchen.

'Your sister is turning me into a food-dependent man,' he said to me. 'These days if I don't eat her food for six hours I began to suffer withdrawal symptoms.'

On her way out of the kitchen Ego thanked him very much for his compliment, laughed, waved her arms about, and took a seat facing her husband.

After lunch, Ezendu took charge of me. We went over to a long, softly lit room in a corner of his mansion. It had a long, crammed bar, ageing leather sofas, shelves full of long playing records, CDs and cassettes and a music centre that covered most of one wall. He produced two glasses and a chilled bottle of champagne from the bar and filled the glasses, then he searched the shelves for a long while, selected a pile of CDs and put one on. The Marvin Gaye classic *Let's do it again* came on. He fussed with the remote control buttons until he got the volume and sound quality he wanted.

He began by counselling me. Black Americans, he said with venom, were to be avoided completely. They were lazy, dishonest, dissolute, grasping; in short they had all the vices known to mankind and apparently not one single virtue.

'Many of our boys get involved with black American women, but that is a dangerous mistake which you must avoid at all costs,' he said, staring into my eyes to emphasise the point.

I hadn't slept with a woman for months and was even seriously considering abandoning the only taboo I had where sleeping with women is concerned: i.e. never to go with prostitutes. So I was amused by Ezendu's advice that I avoid African-American women, but I didn't say a word. Ezendu wasn't an easy man to disagree with. He had an absolutist air about him, and I listened with total attention, giving him his due as a fellow countryman who had lived in America for more than twenty years and had made a great deal of money, someone who had earned the right to hand down advice to everyone else and be listened to.

'Never ever even think of marrying a black American woman. Don't even dream of it. I have given this advice to many people; some refused to listen and they are paying for it now.'

On the wall directly opposite me was a large poster of Sidney Poitier receiving some award. We were listening to Marvin Gaye on the CD player and the LPs on the shelves whose sleeves I could make out from my seat were all by African-Americans: Ella Fitzgerald, Roberta Flack, Ray Charles. It seemed that these African-Americans – successful actors and musicians – did not merit Ezendu's condemnation. Or maybe their music and their films were excepted but not their persons.

Ezendu didn't like white people much either. They were a load of racists, only marginally better than African-Americans.

'When I was working in LA,' he said, 'a white woman was brought in for emergency surgery and I was checking her in with a young white doctor who worked under me. This woman said, right there in front of me, that she hoped they were not going to let me into the room when she was being operated on. I was the best surgeon in that hospital by a mile. And that woman said that in front of a young white doctor who worked for me.'

He paused and his eyes drifted away for a while. He had wanted to kill that woman and had had to struggle to contain himself, Ezendu said, at length. He went outside and smoked cigarettes to calm himself down. But that woman was even better than the hidden type, he said, those ones who pretend to be your

127

friends but their minds were always plotting to undermine you. You had to be on your guard all the time, you had to prove yourself over and over again every day of your life, every minute.

Ezendu paused; he looked like a man who had knife wounds that were forever deepening and widening. The contrast between his big beautiful house, his young beautiful wife, his stash of money, all his wonderful possessions and this squalid, comprehensive bitterness was startling. And I wondered: wasn't his kind of success supposed to free one, at least in part, from that kind of bitterness? When you had fought all those battles and won the big house and the two new cars and the stack of credit cards, could you not see that those you felt were always trying to undermine you were merely being as pathetic as human beings tend to be all over the world and look upon them with some pity, even some compassion? Or perhaps that all the enemies you saw in every corner were merely reflections of your own insecurity and alienation? If success didn't give you that little bit of confidence, didn't allow you to let down your guard from time to time, then what was it worth?

After a long silence, Ezendu turned his attention to Nigeria, as if he needed to get away from America. He grilled me minutely about the state of the country when I left it and the news I'd heard by phone from my parents and friends, but it became increasingly clear that he had more current information about Nigeria than I did. His passion was politics, which even when I was in Nigeria was of little more than passing interest to me. After satisfying himself that he had extracted all the information I had about Nigeria, he declared that the country's political leaders were all morons, a view which is widely held but one which he expressed with more feeling than anyone else I've ever met.

'I'm planning to visit Nigeria soon,' he said. 'In fact I'm considering moving there to settle sometime in the future, but

I'm going to play an active part in politics even before I go back to settle finally. All these politicians don't know what they are doing. I can't wait for a chance to give them a piece of my mind.'

Then he outlined, by speech and energetic gesticulation, a series of political strategies, consisting in the main of ethnic realignments, with which he hoped to transform Nigerian politics. Ezendu's strategies were so complicated they sounded to me like theories of nuclear physics. The reality I knew was much simpler: a few so-called leaders, waving the ethnic banner, struck deals all the time with whoever happened to hold or want political power and they were handsomely paid for their trouble. Ethnic politics was good business; the ethnic groups were political commodities whose prices changed seasonally, like farm produce. A shrewd politician was one who knew when to hoard and when to sell.

As Ezendu bombarded me with his far-fetched strategies for ethnic fusions and fissions, and scenarios for terrible explosions, I tried to listen and look intelligent, but the heavy lunch and my host's excellent champagne had dulled my intellect and, much to my subsequent embarrassment, I soon fell asleep.

◆

Ezendu forgave me for falling asleep on that occasion, while his political passions were in flow, and I was invited to his beautiful house once a month and drank more of his champagne. One rainy, cold Saturday afternoon in February, expectancy hung like a thick fog in the Ezendus' living room. At Ezendu's prompting, a colleague of his at the hospital he worked in had arranged for a local Republican politician, Prime, to call on the Ezendus for drinks. For Ezendu this was meant to be a first step on the ladder to acquiring political influence, maybe even public office.

The white walls of the living room and the severe modernist

furniture had been thoroughly polished as though to erase all evidence of human habitation from the house. Two long tables in the dining area were laden: one with spirits, wines, liqueurs and beers, the other with pies, cutlets, kebabs and Nigerian delicacies – bowls of fish and lamb pepper soup whose brown uninteresting appearance concealed the tropical-pepper fires that burned in them. Ego had sensibly stuck little red signs on the Nigerian dishes that warned: 'very hot'. Dressed in a dark blue skirt suit and a collarless shirt of thin light blue stripes, she had the look of a powerful corporate attorney on her way to court. Ezendu was turned out in a bold black and white check sports jacket and black trousers. His white shirt was clearly being worn for the first time; his tie had lucid abstract patterns in blue, white and red like a painting by Mondrian. Ezendu's friend, Ibeanu, a man of dried-stockfish features who worked in a San Francisco firm of accountants, wore a new brown suit. I thought I heard the rustle of the label each time he moved his left arm. Another friend of Ezendu's, Ogbu, a businessman, nearly as enormous as Ezendu but with a nicer softer face, wore a cream *agbada* with extravagant gold embroidery and several strings of red beads. His wife was in a *boubou* of the same cloth as the *agbada*, also heavily embroidered; she, too, had her own load of beads. I looked unforgivably casual in short sleeves and trousers. No one had told me to dress like someone attending a wedding.

To my astonishment Uncle Happiness arrived with a flourish, swimming inside a huge jumper and skirt made of a hand-woven fabric of black, deep orange and violet designs. He had a stack of CDs and audio tapes under his arm. He bellowed from the door: 'I know I'm late, God forgive me. My car refused to start, I did everything but the son-of-a-harlot just wouldn't start. I had given up, I was on my way back to the house to call a taxi, and I said, let me just try the car one more time, and do you know what happened? It started just like that. One try. All the car wanted to do was to make me late; I beg your forgiveness. May God slice off that useless car's ears.'

His apologies still running, he went round the room hugging everyone there, struggling to keep his CDs from falling on the floor. I hadn't seen or spoken to him since the day I found out that he had conned me out of two hundred dollars for the forged social security card. When he came to me, he shouted: 'Obi, my son! You don't even bother to phone your uncle. I know you are very busy, but try and call once in a while. I worry so much about you.' Then lowering his voice, he said: 'This is my new line of business' (patting his CDs). 'I play high quality music, African and other types, at important occasions. I will be making lots of money very soon.'

I wondered to myself how many lines of business Uncle Happiness had tried in his twenty-five years in America, how many dead ends he had zoomed into full of hope.

'Do you know he is my elder sister's son?' Happiness asked of everyone in the room before taking leave of me. Ezendu watched him with a look of irritation; others wore smiles of amusement. Happiness established himself behind the stereo set on a table in a corner of the dining area, and soon filled the room with an old *soukous* tune by Franco. The beat made something inside your head sway involuntarily from side to side, making you gently tipsy. It is difficult to describe how wonderful African music sounds in America. I hadn't even heard of Franco when I was in Nigeria, but in my five months here, I had acquired, at great cost, an extensive *soukous* CD collection, in addition to *juju* and *highlife*; like a man who had had to travel to a distant land in order to discover his home.

I noticed that even Ezendu moved to the music while checking on everything, a battle commander on a last-minute tour of his defences. Ogbu, Ibeanu and I were seated around the living room

131

on polished chairs, admiring the polished walls in lieu of conversation, Ego and Mrs Ogbu were in the dining area chatting nervously, Ezendu was for the third time re-arranging the wines and liqueurs when the doorbell rang.

Ezendu went to answer it, moving extremely slowly: he didn't want to appear nervous, but it seemed as if his brain had substantially lost contact with his limbs.

Prime was a tall, spare man with rich brown and grey eyebrows and moustache that pointed in all directions. He wore an old navy blue sweater and faded jeans; his tiny wife, whose head barely reached his shoulders, was draped in a brightly patterned blanket-like top that looked like something from Guatemala, over black jeans.

Ezendu led his guests to where we stood waiting to receive them, his face showing signs of severe injury, as if Prime and his wife had insulted him by being so casually dressed.

The Primes shook hands all round. Vicki, the wife, struggled to pronounce each person's name the right way, ran her hands over Mrs Ogbu's *boubou*, declared that Happiness's outfit was stunning and enquired from him where she could get a CD of the *soukous* tune that throbbed from the loudspeakers. My uncle went into a long, uncoordinated story about the CD which Ezendu cut short by steering the Primes to the hors d'oeuvres and drinks tables. Prime carefully picked a few shrimps and a chicken pie after careful examination. His wife opted for fish pepper soup.

'It's a bit hot,' Ego warned her.

'I think I can handle it,' Vicki said. We all watched nervously as she stirred the small bowl of pepper soup Ego had served her and put half a spoonful to her lips. Her face tensed with struggle; for a moment I thought she would eject the soup into Ezendu's worried face, but she somehow got it down, exhaled loudly, shook her head and said, 'Whoo! This thing packs a punch!'

Everyone laughed with relief.

Ezendu, Ogbu, Ibeanu and I stood around Prime in the centre of the living room; Vicki was showing a lot of interest in Happiness, and she and the other women stood beside him discussing something which brought out a lot of Happiness's bellowing laughter.

'John is one of the leading businessmen from Nigeria on the West Coast. He's heavily involved in international trade,' Ezendu said to Prime, indicating Ogbu. 'Mike,' he said, referring to the accountant, 'is a highly experienced CPA. His office is on Market Street in the city, and Obi is an economic analyst for many Nigerian companies doing business in the States. We're all active in the organisation of African immigrants resident in California. John, Mike and I are on the executive committee; Obi is one of the leaders of the youth movement.'

Prime nodded several times, seemingly very impressed. As far as I knew there was no organization of African immigrants resident in California, and I was surprised to learn that I was an economic analyst, not a security guard. I avoided Ezendu's eyes and looked at the floor.

'We are in touch with all the other immigrant organisations here and in other parts of the States,' Ezendu went on. 'We hold meetings regularly and we are developing strategies to promote our common interests.'

'Sounds pretty good,' Prime said.

'Most immigrants,' Ezendu said, 'are very hardworking and resourceful. As you may know, all over the States there are hundreds of thousands of doctors and engineers and accountants and economists and businessmen originally from Africa and Asia.'

'I hear,' Prime volunteered, 'that a lot of the folks in Silicon Valley are of Chinese and Vietnamese descent.'

'You are exactly right, and there are thousands of doctors from India, Egypt and Nigeria,' Ezendu added.

'In fact,' Ibeanu said, 'in some hospitals all the doctors are immigrants.'

Throwing a frown at Ibeanu for what he must have thought an ill-considered statement, Ezendu quickly said, 'I'm not sure Mike is correct. Immigrant doctors are a significant minority, but a minority nonetheless.'

Ibeanu swallowed the rebuke quietly, his eyes full of apology.

'The entire immigrant population is one hundred per cent conservative,' Ezendu continued. 'We work hard – we believe that everybody should – and we have very strong family values. We believe that our natural home is in the Republican Party.'

Ezendu paused to check the effect of what he had said. His forehead was stetched taut by anxiety; the need to know if he was making an impact had doubled the size of his nose. His moustache stood on edge; his lips trembled. Prime's expression was neutral, as though his mind were preoccupied with matters far away from that room.

'What I'm trying to say,' Ezendu went on more strenuously, 'is that we want to develop close links with the Republican Party, to support it in any way we can. This is a critical period in the history of this country, and we want to make our little contribution to seeing that it moves in the right direction.'

'Hmm,' Prime said, nodding slowly, the distant expression still on his face. I noticed that Ogbu looked rather uneasy. He exported containers of California wine to Nigeria and imported Nigerian nurses to work in the US; he was also said to hold a few McDonald franchises. He had a large home in Half Moon Bay and six children, two of whom were in good colleges. I suspected that he wasn't sure this dabbling in American politics was a good idea. It might have seemed to him like telling a man who has generously given you a roof over your head that you wanted to sleep with his wife.

'I strongly believe there will be mutual benefits in our working together,' Ezendu said. 'We can contribute money and time, and people. And when there are any issues on which we feel strongly, we will let you know.'

'We have many capable people,' said Ibeanu trying, I thought, to make up for his earlier gaffe, 'capable people like Dr Ezendu, who is very influential among all immigrants throughout the country.'

'Hmm,' Prime said, 'excellent.'

But it wasn't clear what, if anything, was excellent. Prime seemed to want to maintain absolute blankness towards what he was being told. He appeared to belong to that breed of politicians who are neither conservative nor liberal nor even centrist, but who float in a balloon of cautious ambition above all political positions and commitments.

'I believe Newt Gingrich is an extraordinarily remarkable man,' Ezendu said. 'I have followed the Republican revolution in Congress every inch of the way, and I am a fanatical supporter. I think Newt and others are on the verge of changing America forever.'

I thought I detected a subtle frown on Prime's face at the mention of Gingrich, but Ezendu went on affirming his faith in that revolution and its extraordinarily remarkable helmsman. When he paused, Prime glanced at his watch, said nothing.

'We are opposed to illegal immigration,' Ezendu continued, in full swing, 'I fully support Governor Wilson. There should be a strictly controlled process of immigration. America is not the world's Father Christmas.'

Prime remained resolutely non-committal, playing it very safe, the way he had earlier on avoided the peppery Nigerian delicacies on offer. The Republican politicians Ezendu was invoking seemed too peppery for Prime's palate.

What amazed me was for how long, in the face of Prime's unyielding reticence, Ezendu kept up his pledges of loyalty, his arguments about mutual benefits, his declaration that the Republican Party was the natural home for all immigrants. He was an incredibly thick-skinned suitor blind to a hundred different hints that he wasn't wanted.

As if the evening wasn't going badly enough for Ezendu, we were all suddenly drawn by Happiness's bellows as he left his disc jockey's table and began dancing to a *highlife* tune, *Sweet Mother*. Prime, taking advantage of a pause, quickly detached himself from our group to get a better view of the dance, grateful for the distraction. Ezendu muttered something under his breath; I glanced at him and quickly looked away. His large face emitted a dangerous anger: I wondered how much of that anger was caused by my Uncle Happiness and how much by a country that, after all Ezendu's years here, still had the capacity to confound him.

Prime and the women formed a ring around Happiness and began clapping to the beat of the music. Happiness threw his trunk left and right and stomped on the floor and rotated his arms above his head like a windmill. I wanted to draw closer, but out of loyalty to Ezendu, I (and Ogbu and Ibeanu) watched from the living room while trying to pretend lack of interest.

Powered by the clapping, by little shouts of encouragement, by the ever-rising tide of the music, Happiness's dancing grew wilder, the gaping smile on his face wider. He jerked his pelvis forwards and backwards, passionately copulating with air, and then he threw himself forward and landed at the feet of Prime's wife, who was one of the most enthusiastic spectators. With an unsteady curtsey he asked her for a dance. 'Oh sure,' she said, and joined him in the centre of the ring, her blanket top flapping about. Uncle Happiness began to sing in his bellowing tone alongside the *highlife* singer:

> Sweet Mother, I no go forget you
> for the suffer wey you suffer for me
>
> If a no sleep, my mother no go sleep
> If a no chop, my mother no go chop
>
> She no dey tire o!

His pelvis moved with a fluidity incredible in such an overweight body. Vicki matched him thrust for thrust, wiggle for wiggle, laughing torrentially; she was having so much fun it seemed to make her cry. Happiness abandoned the pelvic dance and began bending down as though to pick up something from the floor and then straightening up swiftly. Vicki followed his lead but couldn't match Happiness's suppleness. They circled around each other with mock wariness, bending down and rising rapidly as they went. Happiness changed the dance yet again. This time he stood on a spot and trembled slowly from head to toe as though he were made of jelly. That was beyond Vicki and she had to content herself with standing in front of him and shaking her body from side to side.

After a long while, perhaps at a furtive signal from her husband, Vicki announced between greedy swallows of air that they had to leave – another appointment to catch.

'You're just too much,' she told Happiness, boxing his shoulder. He answered with a wide grin and a low bow, and continued dancing. The Primes shook hands all round, said they'd had a wonderful time. Ezendu and Ego saw them off while the rest of us continued watching Happiness swaying, shaking and twirling to *Sweet Mother*, dripping sweat. He must have made a special lengthy tape of the song for each time it seemed about to come to an end it started all over again. I noticed two empty bottles of

Piper Sonoma standing beside Happiness's disc jockey's table, and I surmised that large quantities of sparkling wine had contributed significantly to his exuberance and fluidity.

With both hands he lifted his right leg and hopped about on the left one, managing at the same time to gently sway from side to side. Then he lifted the left leg and hopped about on the right one. Even when Ezendu, back from seeing off his guests, stood only a few feet away from Happiness and cast embittered eyes at him, Happiness didn't miss a beat. Instead he called out to his audience breathlessly: 'Come and join me! Don't let this wonderful music go to waste, I beg you all in the name of God.'

No one joined him, but he didn't really need any support. He became a boatman, his arms swinging backwards and forwards as he paddled an imaginary boat, then he bent low from his waist and began to cut grass with an imaginary machete while tapping the floor with his feet in time with the music, then he became a traffic policeman furiously directing traffic.

Uncle Happiness seemed able to turn life's laws upside down, to defiantly seize a euphoric joy which did not rightly belong to him. There was something enviable about his ability to pluck happiness out of thin air like a conjurer (albeit with the help of sparkling wine), his ability to throw away the cares of this world like used toilet paper. But with time that joy began to show signs of strain. His wide smile began to fade: he was returning to the bleakness of the present. It struck me at that moment that for all the time he had spent in this country, Happiness had, in a sense, never arrived in America. His soul had never learnt (was perhaps incapable of learning) how to exist within the confines of long term plans, how to follow doggedly the immigrant's mountainous path to success. His body, thrashing about like a huge, wounded python, seemed trapped in the temperament of a different climate, a land of perpetual sunshine.

He did a sudden pirouette and then flung himself up into the air. He didn't get very far before returning to earth with a heavy thud that almost made the mansion shiver. He executed another pirouette and threw himself up again, and this time he barely left the floor.

The Monster With Fifty Heads

It rained all through February. On local TV there were nightly stories of floods and power cuts all over the Bay Area; mighty sinkholes appeared behind some of San Francisco's pretty old houses and threatened to swallow them up. I wore two shirts and two sweaters to work and, bloated under my coat like a corpse, I stuck my face to the windscreen of my little Corolla, peering through fog thick as pap which rearranged the beam of your headlights into rolls of fine gauze blocking your way, through a murky darkness that fell suddenly in the afternoon the way a power cut happened back in Nigeria. Andrew had paid stiff electricity bills in his first winter in America so he was stingy with the heating, and though I slept under a pile of blankets, my nose flowed like a stream and my sides hurt so much that pneumonia was very much on my mind. It was little consolation that this Bay Area winter was child's play compared to the snow-covered East Coast and Midwest.

Lying under my blankets on my one free day a week, staring through the window of Andrew's room at long thin grains of falling rain, I missed home more than I thought possible. Robo's thin-fingered touch, her unhurried, meandering laugh, her bra-free jiggling breasts. Lagos – the lagoon, blue and wonderful, the city free of chaos, bad temper and violence, filth and evil smells, the nightclubs filled to the brim with beautiful people, energy and good cheer at full throttle – a Lagos that existed only in my cold, homesick mind. My ageless mother, rippling with strength, leading the women in church in an almost erotic, buttock-shaking dance of thanksgiving to the Lord at the services I attended once in a while. My gorgeous younger sister, Nwaka, going through some of the most confusing years of her life without the counsel of her big bro. Over and over I asked myself: What are you doing here, for God's sake? Why can't you just go home and get any kind of job? As if jobs littered the streets of Lagos.

My spirits lifted as the sun began its return in March. Though I could barely afford it, I found a place of my own, positioning myself to take advantage of the possibilities which I once again sensed were in the air all around me.

'I'm going to miss you,' Andrew said sheepishly, with a look of mourning, as we were moving my things to my car. Because he had given me a roof over my head for eight months, I didn't burst out laughing.

We had rarely had anything to say to each other in all the months I'd stayed in his place. In fact we'd seen very little of each other because of our different working hours – which had suited me just fine.

'I'm going to be just two streets away, Andrew,' I said.

'This country is a funny place,' he said. 'Everybody is so busy. There was a boy from my area who stayed here with me when he first came over. He lives in Hayward now and he hasn't phoned me even once.'

'I'll come and visit you regularly, especially on Sundays,' I said. 'This place will always be my home.'

That brought a smile to his square, ugly face.

'You're right,' he said. 'This place will always be your home.

Please try to come at least once every two weeks, and I will come and see you every weekend.'

'Sure,' I said, though I knew it would never happen. I carried my last case of books down to my car, Andrew behind me bearing my radio-cassette player, looking very sad.

He tried to visit me several times, but I always told him I was rushing off somewhere to see someone urgently and that I would call him as soon as I got back home. I never did call him. After trying for a couple of months, he gave up. I never stepped into his place again. It wasn't just simple ingratitude or unkindness: solidarity among the marginalised and miserable I find very depressing – I didn't want any part of Andrew's bleak life and I didn't wish to share mine with anyone.

My new home was a studio apartment in a huge redbrick building, which looked like one medieval castle placed on top of another. It was on Bellevue Street, less than half a mile from Andrew's place. It had an ancient lift and the corridor to my floor was so poorly lit that whenever I got out of the lift, it felt as though I had descended into a mine shaft, not climbed five floors up. During my first few weeks there I left the fluorescent light in my apartment on all day long, in spite of my terror of high utility charges, because after the semi-darkness of the corridor, a dark room would have been too much to bear.

Most of the time the corridors and the lobby downstairs were empty, even in the morning when you expected a lot of people to be on their way to work at roughly the same time. But from my room I heard distant music and footfalls and the barking and shrieking that accompanied husband/wife, boyfriend/girlfriend quarrels, usually followed by the crash of breaking glass or a car racing off. Over time I saw a few faces frequently enough outside the building and in the lobby to conclude that they lived there: a pudgy, bespectacled woman whose boyfriend – a squat and

141

stocky chain-smoking man with a rolling walk like my Uncle Happiness – seemed to take off from time to time and had to be found and brought back, like a straying dog. There was a giant in a big black hat with a white band who always boomed a greeting at me: 'How yu duin' today, brother?'; and a small and lean dark brown man, with scanty, wiry hair, always in a dark blue uniform, a peaked, possibly chauffeur's, cap under his arm. The other twenty-six or so occupants of the block of apartments, listed on a board beside the entrance, seemed to be phantoms.

The floor of my apartment was of shiny red wood; it made an annoying thunking sound as you walked across the room. The bathroom, though freshly painted, had a number of yellow patches, stains so old and deep they showed through the paint; the bathroom fittings looked at least fifty years old. And there was something painfully meagre and lonely about that long room with the narrow bed, low bedside table and cases of books, and my parents' yellowing wedding picture, a fifteen-year-old photograph of my sisters and me, a large colour portrait of Robo and an old dark poster of Miles Davis. Yet having my own place, having my surname in capital letters on the board beside the entrance to the building, having my own phone and my own letter box gave me a sense of anchoredness which I hadn't felt for a very long time.

◆

The Hook appeared in my apartment about two weeks after I had moved in, and prostrated all six feet three of himself on my wooden floor though he was wearing a new-looking white jogging outfit.

'Oh-bye, I won't get up until you tell me to,' he said. 'I'm sure you can't believe that I've behaved like this to you, so if you tell me to lie down here till next year I will obey you.'

In spite of myself I began to laugh. Back in our university, the Hook was always bashing his head against walls to show how upset he was with his brain for failing to remember the promises he made and broke all the time, or dashing across busy streets, nearly getting himself killed, to hug a friend who had been away from the campus for a week or less. I told him he could get up, and he rose, thanked me for being so lenient with him and then crushed me in a suffocating hug, yelling: 'Oh-bye! Oh-bye! Oh-bye!' like an unhinged football fan.

He was no longer as slim as he had been the last time I saw him, but he still had the handsome unblemished face that many girls in our university had fallen for, to their cost. His breath and the redness of his eyes said he was still a heavy drinker. When he finally let go of me, he jumped on my bed, instantly at home, and declared that my studio apartment was nice, though the eyes with which he looked around seemed to say the opposite.

'Oh-bye, you won't believe what happened,' he said, shifting about on the bed restlessly as he spoke. 'I was very busy, up to my neck in business the day I got your message about your flight. In fact it was from my hotel room in Miami that I accessed my answering machine and heard you say you were going to be here in two days. Men, did I panic? I couldn't just leave Miami; it was the kind of deal you do once in a lifetime, so I almost went mad thinking about what to do. I remembered you'd said you guys no longer lived in your place in Yaba and you didn't have a phone yet in the new place. If there had been a phone, I would have called and told you to fly straight from JFK to Miami. Then I remembered one chick I'd been having something with about that time. Her name was Fiona, big tits; that's what used to drive me crazy about her, massive tits. But she was a greedy chick. Some of the babes here are as greedy as what you get in Nigeria, even worse, as you've probably found out already. It had been the chick's birthday before I left for Miami and I'd just done a really good deal, a really, really good deal, and had some cash, and I wanted to spoil her, because that chick could ball, men. She used to make me shout, you know, like Bronzo used to shout; yell like I was going out of my mind, and I wanted to make her feel good. So, I gave her a thousand bucks to buy something for herself. You know, this bitch wasn't impressed. Didn't even say thank you. She'd seen the bread I made – it was quite a lot – but for God's sake I wasn't going to give her all the money I made in a deal just because she could fuck. No way. So, I got pissed off with her and we quarrelled.'

He paused to swallow half of the can of beer I'd served him, then stared into my eyes as though to compel belief through a kind of semi-hypnotism. Then he took off again: 'When I was thinking of what to do about you I called her and apologised and told her I would give her another thousand bucks once I got back, but even that wasn't enough. That girl is greedy. You know how much she wanted? Can you guess? Five grand, almost all the whole fucking money I made, but we finally agreed I would give her three. Then I gave her the time of arrival of your flight and told her to pick you up and take you to my place and get you settled in because, men, that deal in Miami was hot and I didn't know when I'd leave the place. You won't believe it, but I just got back last week, since July last year. That Fiona bitch has a hot younger sister and some wild friends, and she promised she would get you some action and take real good care of you. So I relaxed, thinking my man was cool. It was when I accessed my voicemail about a couple of weeks after and got all those messages that I started crying. You, staying with Andrew? Andrew, that nerd, that lunatic. Oh my God, I said, that loony is going to drive my man out of his mind. That Fiona bitch, when I see her I'm gonna kill her, I swear to God. I really couldn't call you at Andrew's because what I was involved in was very very sensitive, I'll tell you more about it sometime. I kept thinking I would be back soon and get you away from that monster. And look at me, almost eight months later. I'm so ashamed of myself I want to crawl under your bed and hide. Once I got your address from Andrew, I couldn't wait to call you, I just rushed down here immediately.'

The sums of money he had thrown into the air like balls – one thousand bucks, five grand, three – and the secret lucrative business deals he hinted at all had a hollow ring, like the extravagant claims of an inept con artist. His story about being tied up in Miami on business for months and not being able to make phone calls also sounded so false I waved it aside mentally. And the name Fiona seemed to have been taken from one of the porn magazines – *Probe, Mayfair, Hot Confessions,* etc. – which all of us had subscribed to in our teens. All the same it was good to see an old friend after months of loneliness and it wasn't unlikely that he knew some beautiful women with lovely sisters and friends.

We talked about old times. About when we were both stranded on campus at the end of a semester because we had both sold the return air tickets our parents had provided and he'd had to pretend to fall in love with the richest and least attractive girl at the university to get the money for our tickets out of her. About the day he was making out with a girl in his elder sister's car outside the now-defunct Lagos nightclub, Sunrise, and a group of policemen arrested him and threatened to take him and the girl (without her skirt) to the police station. He had come into the nightclub barefooted – because the policemen, though they were holding the car and the girl, had also taken his shoes hostage – to raise a loan of two hundred naira from Robo and me to buy his freedom. About old friends back home who had got married or rich or had moved to England or Germany or died in car accidents or at the hands of armed robbers. About who was going out with who these days, which Lagos nightclubs were rocking, which ones were dying.

'Damn!' he yelled suddenly, looking at his watch, 'I almost forgot I made an appointment to see someone.'

He flew off the bed and ran for the door. I followed him, disorientated.

'Do you have plans for tonight?' he asked at the door.

'Not really,' I said.

'Even if you had plans, now I'm here you have to give me priority. I'm taking some friends and business partners out to a nightclub – Geoffrey's. You have to come with us. Do you know Geoffrey's?'

I shook my head.

'Oh my God, you don't know Geoffrey's? I'm to blame. Putting you at the mercy of that Andrew. Good Lord! Anyway, we're gonna catch up on all that lost time starting tonight. I'll pick you up at eleven on the dot. You'll have to be ready in good time because I'm picking up the others from all over the place and you're nearest to the club, so once I get here you join us and we roll. It's one of those dress code places – jacket, formalish wear, that kind of thing.'

And he ran through the door, talking rapidly about how I must have had an awful time at that Andrew's place and blaming himself for my travails, promising in the dark, old lift that now we had linked up we were going to have a wild time. 'This America is sweet like honey,' the Hook said, 'when you are with people like me.'

He had come in a new aquamarine four-wheel-drive, a Toyota Land Cruiser with hefty tyres that looked like they would weigh heavier than a two-storey home. He unlocked the doors by remote control, still making rapid promises, cursing poor Andrew and his lunatic born-again Christianity. He swung the door open and leapt up from the pavement on to the driver's seat and with tyres screeching, he was gone the next instant, yelling through the window: 'Geoffrey's is formal wear! Remember, formal wear! . . .'

146

I was dazed. Could it be that the Hook's tales of heavy business deals and massive-titted women were not completely false? That he had somehow made enough money to afford that stunning four-wheel drive? That his air of swaggering affluence was not just theatre?

My bleak life got several times bleaker in that moment, as miserable as a slow death from cancer. On the one side, my graveyard-shift job at the warehouses, my fourteen-year-old toy car, my apartment with yellowed bathroom walls and rusty plumbing, my utter womanlessness; on the other hand, the Hook's aquamarine four-wheel-drive and his fashionable Reebok sneakers. The contrast was acutely painful. And I couldn't comfort myself with the thought that the Hook's apparent affluence would somehow rub off on me over time. I had a premonition he wasn't coming back. His entry had been so sudden, his exit so whirlwindy that it all seemed like a mirage. I resented him for trampling all over my life, which I had managed at times to delude myself wasn't too bad and was likely to get better (gradually); for exposing all its drabness. I went back in and took the lift down into the darkness of my mine-shaft apartment, shrunken and desolate. I had been looking forward to watching my countryman, Akeem Olajuwon, in a basketball match that evening, but when I got in, I turned off my TV, lay sideways on my bed and stared at the wooden floor.

But a little bit of hope that the Hook would return and we would go out to a nightclub stuck to the corners of my mind. At ten I pulled out two of my best suits from my wardrobe and laid them on the bed, asking myself all the time why I was bothering, that of course the Hook wasn't going to come back. I was like a much-wounded fifteen-year-old girl who fights with her sensible side over whether to get ready for a date with a lover who has stood her up numerous times in the past. Months of hamburgers, pizzas, ice creams, muffins, sodas and beers had turned my waistline into a mound of flab. The trousers of my suits were so tight that wearing them for thirty minutes would probably have damaged some vital organ inside me so I ironed my newest khaki. Dressing up again after such a long time felt like suddenly discovering you were still fluent in a special language you thought you'd long forgotten. I looked splendid in my dark blue Canali jacket, a zingingly white shirt, a silly colourful tie covered with cartoon men and women in various stages of undress and my soft black leather Gucci shoes. I dabbed myself with *Red for Men* from a bottle I had bought in London in 1992 but which was still half-full. I looked and felt so good that I told myself that if the Hook did not turn up I would take myself out anyway to one of the nightclubs whose addresses I had copied from the papers, or even try to find Geoffrey's on my own. This was America after all and if you tried hard enough you could find anywhere.

By eleven-thirty the Hook hadn't come, and I decided I was going to give him thirty more minutes max. and then if he still didn't show up I'd make other plans. He pounded on my door about ten minutes later and let himself in. He wore a superb black double-breasted suit and a long red fez cap and twirled a slim black walking stick; he looked like a Middle Eastern pasha of the last century.

'Let's go, let's go! Oh you're looking deadly, boy!' he shouted, in a great hurry.

Downstairs there was another aquamarine Land Cruiser parked behind the one the Hook had come with in the afternoon. Gangsta rap pounded the otherwise quiet street from the two vehicles. The street lights revealed the outline of processed hair and female faces in the first Land Cruiser, and my heart went out of control. The Hook opened the rear door of the first one for me and leapt into the driver's seat. There were three young women in the vehicle, one beside him in front, two at the back, and the interior was filled with perfume.

148

'Carol, Rhonda and em (some other name I can't remember) meet Oh-bye, my best friend for more than fifteen years, from way back in Nigeria,' the Hook said, as he swung into the road.

The girls chorused friendly greetings; I replied, very nervous. They were all well turned out; the one beside me – Rhonda – wore a top that consisted of rows of criss-crossing black straps underneath which her breasts thrust forward like bunched fists.

'Oh-bye is a great guy,' the Hook said. 'Any time I got into trouble back home, he was always there for me, like a brother. And all the women loved him. Damn! This guy did things to them they never even dreamt about, drove them right outta their minds. Oooh, they were crazy for my man!'

The girls threw back their heads and laughed as though they were in a competition to see who would laugh loudest. I laughed too, swept along, though still disorientated and nervous.

'Oh, he looks it,' Rhonda said, nudging me flirtatiously.

'Don't mind him,' I said, still laughing. 'He's the one that drove all the girls crazy.'

I couldn't let myself hope I was going to end up in bed with any of these hot women, that my life was on the verge of miraculous transformation, but their perfumes were all over me, the part of my shoulder where Rhonda had nudged me felt warm and tingly. It wasn't a dream at all.

We were outside the nightclub in ten minutes, the Hook chattering all the way, swinging his head from side to side to the hip-hop beat from the car's powerful stereo system. In those ten minutes he told the girls of how I had run a gambling joint in Lagos for three years until I was forced to close it down by a Lagos crime family that sounded in every respect as deadly as a Colombian drug cartel. How I'd wanted to raise my own army of toughs to fight the gang, how he had pleaded with me not to get involved in spilling blood, to come to America instead and try and get into a new line of business. How I was still looking around trying to decide what to get into, how he hoped we'd both get into business together because I was one of the smartest Nigerians alive. The story sounded a bit too fictitious, but I noticed that Rhonda seemed to be looking at me with increased interest. You never knew what worked in these situations, I said to myself.

Outside the club, two men jumped out from the other Land Cruiser. One was a cheap-thriller-gangster type, broad-shouldered in a black suit wearing shiny dark glasses, the other a tall fellow also in a black suit who kept staring at his shoes. There was a long line of well dressed men and women outside the club, at least a block long. I'd never seen so many well turned out people queueing for anything and being so orderly, so meek about it. Stern-looking men in dinner suits, carrying what looked like slim cellular phones, stood at the entrance to the club, checking IDs, patting suits for concealed weapons.

The Hook went over to have a word with the two men who had been in the other Land Cruiser; the three girls clustered together, whispering about something and laughing. I stood to one side, watching them while pretending not to, and I decided that if I was given a choice, I would take Rhonda: the others were prettier and slightly taller, but mine – as I was beginning to think of her – had the most promising body and a mad erotic laugh. His conference with the others over, the Hook led the way into the club. The girls followed behind him, then the two men (who nodded coldly when I said 'Hi' to them); I brought up the rear. We stopped only long enough for the Hook to banter with the men in dinner jackets at the door. They all wanted to know where he had been; Europe on business the last few weeks, he said. It felt good walking straight into the club, past all those poor nicely dressed people waiting patiently in line, and my respect for (and envy of) the Hook grew in leaps and bounds.

We climbed a flight of wide brightly lit stairs, covered with a bright red carpet, and stopped at the broad white door of a private room, marked 'Reserved.' The Hook showed the girls and the three men in, but when it came to my turn, he put a hand on my shoulder and led me away, closing the door with his other hand.

'It's kind of a private business meeting,' he said in an embarrassed tone, 'but I'm gonna join you upstairs later. You can have your pick of any of the other two babes later, the one who sat in front is mine but any of the others you point at is for you.'

He led me upstairs to a crowded dancing hall. A song by Aaliyah was playing deafeningly; even louder than the music was the talking and laughing. The dance floor was packed.

'I'll see you later, very soon; but get their phone numbers,' the Hook whispered fiercely into my ear. 'Dance with them a little then ask if they're married. If they aren't, get their phone numbers. Do it in a nice way. It's very easy.'

And with that piece of advice and encouragement, he gave me a gentle push and ran off to join the others. The atmosphere of the place overwhelmed me, flattened my senses like a bulldozer, stopped me from feeling too bad about how I had been excluded from whatever was going on in the private room downstairs. There were more than two hundred beautiful black women in that room. They covered the entire spectrum from peat black to white, from huge and intimidating to bird-like tininess, all shapes and sizes of breasts, eyes, noses, mouths, smiles. There were a lot of sleeveless, strapless, backless, braless outfits, and the most gorgeous skins in this world were on display.

A tall, dark, slim dish on the dance floor, in a tight red top and a crazy black flared skirt, was slowly pushing her trunk forward until it touched her partner's body, a squat man in a *kente* waistcoat. Then she would hiss, like water sprinkled on a hot iron, and withdraw her body as though she were rearing back to strike, cobra-like, then she would push forward again. A couple were pelvis-bumping madly, looking into each other's half-closed eyes. A tall, slim man slithered up and down his partner's back, whispering something into her ear each time their heads drew level, and she would laugh and slap his writhing waist. Though the beat wasn't exactly what you would call slow, a couple stood still at a corner of the dance floor, wrapped in each other's arms, lost to the world. I walked round the edge slowly, staring, pushing past the people massed around, stepping on people's toes, and no one seemed to mind, or even notice.

Thinking back now, I realise that Geoffrey's that night wasn't much different from a happening Lagos nightclub, but I had spent so many nights in the bleak warehouses on 98th Street and in Andrew's room of religious posters, that a nightclub full of sexy beautiful women affected me like strong wine. Even as I joined the long queue to buy beer from the bar I couldn't tear my eyes away from the dance floor, away from the lovely women chatting and laughing at the top of their voices all around me. Clutching my beer and still staring, I took up a vantage position by the bar, to try and work out a strategy for putting the Hook's advice into action. There were a good number of unattached women, and after a third Heineken, going up to ask one of them for a dance didn't seem like such an uphill undertaking. But I still stood there and watched, telling myself I had to select one that looked least likely to say no, someone who wasn't in a cluster of friends talking, but at the same time it had to be someone reasonably good looking: it would be an abomination to come to such a well endowed place and end up with one of the few unattractive ones. It also had to be someone with a nice, friendly expression, who didn't look bored or frustrated, and I had to make my move when a very danceable tune was playing, preferably something wildly popular, maybe something by Snoop or Aaliyah, so that anyone I asked would be willing to dance.

I was sipping a fifth Heineken and still trying to decide who to approach, still juggling my criteria, when the DJ announced that it was closing time. The next minute the hall was flooded with light. It was barely two a.m. What kind of nightclub closes at two a.m.? I wondered bitterly, as people began streaming towards the staircases.

I joined one of the streams, and on the first floor headed for the private room into which the rest of my party had gone earlier. The room was empty though the Reserved sign still hung on the door. I looked into two other private rooms on the same floor in case I had gone to the wrong one but they were all empty. I sought out one of the tuxedoed employees of the nightclub, and very nicely and patiently, he explained to me that since he had no idea who had been in which private room, he had no way of knowing where they could have gone. I went out into the street. Many of those emerging from the club still hung around waiting for the valet to bring their cars while a few diehard woman-chasers tried to make last minute kills. I very nearly asked one of the doormen if he knew anything about two aquamarine Land Cruisers but stopped myself just in time. I hung by the door, peering desperately at every face. The cars were brought round and the crowd outside dwindled steadily.

By three-fifteen a.m. I and two of the doormen were the only people left on that stretch of 14th Street. I asked about getting a taxi.

◆

Though I hungered day and night for the girl in the strappy dress, I stopped myself from calling the Hook to find out why they had abandoned me at Geoffrey's. I had taken enough shabby treatment from him and I told myself that if he ever called I would let him know exactly what I thought of his behaviour. He did not call.

Two months later Robo told me on the phone that the Hook had suddenly turned up in Lagos the week before. The story going round, Robo said, was that the Hook had fled the US just ahead of an FBI investigation. During a raid on his apartment, which was said to be the Northern California base of a large gang involved in every conceivable kind of fraud, they'd found seven passports, one British, one Jamaican, the others from African countries, a bag full of green and social security cards, and a floppy disk which had the names and addresses of more than two hundred people – Americans, Nigerians, others – out of which about forty had already been conned in the last three years. The gang leader, who had more than fifty identities, like a monster with fifty disposable heads, had been arrested in Los Angeles, and the Hook had been extremely lucky to get away.

I still sometimes wonder if the Hook's invitation to Geoffrey's had been part of a plan to draw me into their gang (which would have failed for I have too little liver to be any sort of criminal), or if he'd genuinely wanted to give an old friend a good time.

Drunken-Driver Love

My sexual fortunes took a turn for the better early in May. It was a great time of year; sunny but cool, Bay Area tourist-brochure weather; but I was in low spirits – still smarting from the way the Hook had treated me, completely fed up with my life that consisted of the depressing warehouses and a host of ever-growing hungers. To make matters worse, my girlfriend, Robo, had said the last time I called her that their firm had major audits in June and July and she wouldn't be visiting then as we'd planned and she wasn't even sure of August. (I learnt later that, as far as she was concerned, it was over between us by then and she knew she wasn't visiting America that year, at least not to see me.) So I must have sounded quite unfriendly when Ego rang me one Saturday afternoon and said she and her husband had been wondering why they hadn't seen or heard from me for a while. I said I'd been busy. Then she said there was someone she wanted me to meet, a girl she knew in Lagos who had moved recently to the Bay Area from Washington D.C. and who'd complained of being lonely.

Disappointments and misery had dulled my faculties and it took me a while to appreciate what Ego was saying. When it registered that I might finally be about to get lucky, even if only with someone from Nigeria (not any of the lovely African-American women I saw driving by on Grand Avenue, or an exotic au pair from Austria), my brain simply rejected that possibility. It was going to be another cruel disappointment – like the Hook's welcoming pussy, like the girl with long brown hair in Cody's Bookshop at Berkeley ('I'm new; I've just come from Africa'), the girl in the strappy dress at the back of the Hook's Toyota Land Cruiser caressing my body with her perfume, the hundreds of women I'd slept with in my increasingly desperate dreams.

'She's a nurse,' Ego was saying. 'She has a very good job and she will soon qualify for a green card. But what she wants is a serious relationship. I know you, Obi, you are such a bad boy, so if you aren't going to treat her well, we'd better just forget it. She's suffered from men in the past and I know how you men are. I don't want her to hold me responsible if you use her and dump her. So, please, I'm begging you, if you are not interested in a serious relationship, let's just forget I called you. She has very good prospects and she's hard-working. She's a very good girl. If you want someone to be serious with, I think she's perfect for you, but if you just want to play around, like you men always do, then let's just leave her alone.'

There had to be someone, otherwise Ego wouldn't be running off her mouth like a bloody preacher. No, there would certainly be a catch. She might be so hideous you would rather die of sexual starvation than have anything to do with her, a face like a hippo, so marriage-crazy you would have to go to the registry office first before you saw her bra. So I set off for the Ezendus' place in Blackhawk, sure that I was stupidly embarking on a futile mission, cursing myself for not telling Ego that I just wasn't interested.

From across the Ezendus' vast living room, as she stood by a window admiring one of the gardens which surrounded the mansion, the nurse who would soon qualify for a green card, who wanted a serious relationship and who had been hurt by a bunch of men in the past, looked quite nice, tall and shapely, in the kind of sleeveless top male models love to pose in, tucked into a pair of faded jeans which did great things to her curves, and a face which didn't look bad at all. But when I drew closer to be introduced, caught now between my uncertainty that there was going to be a huge catch somewhere and the rash excitement of my prick, she looked like an automobile which had been carefully restored after a bad accident but on a tight budget, so that some of the panels were not quite as smooth as they seemed from afar. Her eyes had no character; they waited, like servants, for a cue. When they made contact with mine, they seemed to wilt, like those plants which are averse to sunlight. Her face was full of lines of premature middle age; her voice shook slightly when she spoke; her accent had a high-pitched American super-market put-on pleasantness – you heard the clatter of cash machines in the background and you expected to hear the question: paper or plastic? There was such an air of desperate nervousness about her, such an utter absence of self-confidence. When I gave her my sweetest smile and she looked like she didn't know whether to smile back or run away or take her clothes off, I said to myself that this one would be annoyingly easy. (Considering that I hadn't slept with anyone for nearly ten months and that even successful masturbation could no longer be taken for granted, I wonder now if I really could've thought her 'annoyingly easy' or if hindsight has rewritten my memory.)

Ego orchestrated things with amusing nervousness: stumbling over her words and the furniture in her living room as she invited us to sit down, she put Vivian – that was the nurse's name – on the same three-seater sofa as me, and rushed off to bring drinks for us, then remembered she hadn't asked us what we wanted. She came back and asked us with a nervous laugh, and then mixed things up, bringing a can of Coke for Vivian who had said she wanted orange juice and brandy for me when all I'd asked for was beer.

'When did you come to America?' I asked Vivian, feeling very cool in the midst of all that nervousness.

'Two years ago,' she said, then added apologetically, 'such a long time ago.'

'Two years is very short,' Ego said, leaping to her defence. 'I can't believe you've done so much in two years. Some people spend ten years here working as security guards, and you already have a good job and you have settled down so well.'

For my benefit, Ego added, 'The hospital here offered her almost ten thousand dollars more than she was earning in Washington, and she just made one phone call to them, not even a formal application.'

I winced inwardly at Ego's reference to security guards, but joined her in marvelling at Vivian's meteoric rise.

'It is a bit easier for nurses once you've passed the exams,' she said.

'Even then you have to be willing to work hard; if you were not hard-working they wouldn't have been so anxious to hire you,' Ego said.

I agreed with what Ego was saying. All the while my eyes travelled over Vivian's body. I could see I was making her extremely uncomfortable, and whenever our eyes met she gave me a shy, embarrassed smile and looked around the room as though searching for a hiding place, away from the sexual suggestions my eyes were making.

'So what do you do in your spare time?' I asked, my eyes still groping her body.

The way she shrank away from me, the way her eyes begged for mercy, it seemed as if I'd asked a really dangerous question.

'I write letters home,' she said finally, in a tone of shameful confession, 'and I visit Ego, and I call my friends in Washington.'

'She has only been here two months,' Ego said, ready as ever to act as her friend's defence counsel.

'The Bay Area is a very exciting place to live in,' I said. 'There are plays and music shows and art exhibitions all the time, not just in San Francisco but even in the smallest towns, and there are lots of lovely beaches all over Northern California. There's so much to do here often the problem is finding the time to do all of them.'

The previous September I'd been to the Grand Lake cinema to see *Shawshank Redemption*. I'd probably been the only one in the cavernous theatre who'd come alone and had felt so self-conscious that I hadn't been to see a film or play or anything since then. Apart from that night at the Grand Lake and the night the Hook took me to Geoffrey's, my knowledge of the exciting cultural life of the Bay Area, which I spoke about with so much expansiveness, came entirely from the papers and from radio and TV. But it worked.

'My husband never takes me anywhere,' Ego said miserably.

158

'He's always in surgery or attending conferences all over America. To be married to a doctor is so hard.'

'I acted in some plays in school, but since then I haven't even gone to watch any, I'd like to go sometime though,' Vivian said, then a look of alarm spread over her face; as though she'd said something terribly wrong.

'When next there's something nice I'll let you know,' I said. 'So how was social life in Washington?'

'I went out very rarely,' she said, in her tone of shame, examining her long fingers. 'I worked long hours and I was always tired. My friends took me to the movies once or twice.'

'Vivian,' I said, wagging at finger at her in mock admonition, 'you have to learn to make time to have fun. Life is not all about working hard.'

The effect of that ordinary statement was dramatic: Vivian shook all over the seat with a laughter grossly out of proportion to what I'd just said, managing at the same time to combine her great mirth with great nervousness, and even terror.

I saw admiration in Ego's eyes, they seemed to say: you bad boy, you clearly haven't lost it.

We talked, inevitably, about the bad news from Nigeria. They both said that in spite of everything they were missing home, Ego especially, whose husband was out of town at the time. Remembering home made her gloomy. She went into her kitchen and returned with a dewy bottle of some California champagne. But the champagne didn't improve her mood.

'Surgery and conferences, that's all my husband does. People work so hard in this country you wonder if it's worth it, you wonder what they're working for,' Ego moaned as she went through a second glass.

'Bills, cars, houses, money to send home,' I said, 'then you have children and you want good schools for them, you want to give them good opportunities. That's what it's all about, and it's

159

not safe to wonder if it's worth it. If you start thinking like that you never know where it'll lead to.'

'I am depressed sometimes and miss home, but I'm also very happy to live in America,' Vivian said with unusual vigour, avoiding both our eyes as though afraid she was causing great offence. 'My life here has been useful. I have helped my people back home with the little money I've made. If I had remained in Nigeria, I don't think I would have achieved anything. I'm grateful for America. My life – ' She stopped abruptly as though suddenly feeling she'd said too much already.

'You're right,' Ego said meekly, like a child accepting a parent's reprimand, 'it's just that sometimes you wonder why people have to work so hard in this place.'

'But there are rewards for that hard work,' Vivian said. 'Look at this wonderful house, look at your life. The work is hard, but at least you have something to show for it at the end of the day.'

'Of course, you're right,' Ego said and there was a long silence. I had nothing more to say on the subject, though it occupied my mind a lot of the time. Could any amount of material success justify the loneliness and frustrations of this country and the deformities of character inevitably wrought by those frustrations, by the gigantic loneliness? But was it not even worse back home? Didn't the lack of opportunities produce their own deformities, their own deadly frustrations? How did you make a rational choice?

I left them at about ten p.m. to return to Oakland and to my security guard job at the warehouses, taking Vivian's phone number and promising to call her in a couple of days.

◆

Memory erupted in Vivian's apartment when, on my free day the week after, I went to see her. I sat at one end of her zebra-

160

striped sofa after a wonderful nostalgia-inflaming meal of *garri*, *egusi* and smoked fish, drinking Heineken. She sat at the other end in a sleeveless top and a pair of shorts, sipping Diet Coke and remembering greedily, as if she'd waited all her life for this chance to tell her story. My eyes moved between her face and her bare arms and legs, and she occasionally broke off to examine her body as if checking to make sure my eyes had not bored a hole in her.

'What I miss most are small silly things,' she said, 'like roast corn and coconut. There was a woman who lived next to our compound and sold corn just outside. I miss *her* corn. She knew exactly the kind I liked. She would call out, "Vivi, I have your soft corn, I have been keeping it for you since morning." My sister wrote me last year and said she lost her husband in an accident. I was still in DC then. He left her with five children, all very young, still in secondary school, and no money. She's going to bring up all of them from selling corn by the roadside. I sent her a little money and she wrote a letter of four pages to thank me, and it was just fifty dollars. What will that do for her with all those children? I feel helpless sometimes, so many people suffering back home and there's very little you can do – '

She broke off to check herself and to examine my face, then said, 'I must be boring you.'

'Not at all.'

'Are you sure? Let me know when I become boring.'

'You won't become boring.'

'Did you ever go for a trade fair in Lagos as a child?'

'It's possible my parents took us, but I really can't remember.'

'I loved trade fairs. My uncle's wife sold cosmetics. She always had a stand and my sister and I would go to help her after school. So many people walking around, so many things to look at. We rarely went out of my uncle's house except to go to school or to church so seeing all those people was so wonderful.

My sister and I would just sit at our stand staring at all the different kinds of people.'

After a long pause, 'My uncle's wife was wicked. She would abuse my sister and me: "Useless people, greedy children, how can you eat so much? You spend the whole day eating, eating, eating. Are you pregnant? You can't sweep the floor properly, you can't wash plates. You have power only for eating. Who will marry you?" And everyone said she was very good at bringing up children. We didn't have any choice anyway. Our mother died young, our father has always lived in our village in the east. He is a lazy, idle man and he didn't know what to do with us after our mother died. He remarried, but everyone said his second wife was a witch and would kill us so our mother's brother took us with him to Lagos. Our father and his wife were happy to see us go. My uncle's wife reminded us every chance she got that our mother was dead and our father was lazy and poor and couldn't even feed us if we were sent back to him. She said we were thieves. If anything was misplaced in the house, she said my sister and I had stolen it. She hated my sister because she was tough and sometimes fought back, but she also respected her for that. She called me a coward and a fool because I always tried to avoid trouble for myself and for my sister and was always begging her for forgiveness when she was always the one who wronged us.'

I pictured the younger sister back in Nigeria, a fighter in the face of lousy odds, and I momentarily wished she was the one on the sofa beside me.

'How about your uncle, what did he think about all this?'

'He supported his wife, he kept complaining that he didn't know what devil made him agree to take us. He told us that to our faces several times. We did all the housework in that house and helped in my uncle's wife's shop after school and during holidays. We were their servants. He grumbled when he had to buy anything for us. He said we were bent on finishing his money so he won't be able to bring up his own children. He beat my sister a lot because she had a temper and always got into trouble.'

Vivian had wanted to study medicine in university and had been offered admission, but her uncle said he had no money to pay for a six-year university course, and she'd gone to nursing school instead. 'He didn't want his servant to become a doctor. His wife made fun of me: "You want to go there and disgrace yourself, you don't know it's people from good families who go to university. Who will you tell them is your father? That ignorant villager? You don't know it, but my husband is doing you a favour; he's saving you from big disgrace. Left to me, he should allow you to go there so that you will be exposed once and for all, you thief, you slut." I had done very well in JAMB while her eldest daughter was not even able to get admission into secondary school, and she was only three years younger than me. My sister, who was her age, was already in senior secondary. So my uncle's wife hated us so much at that time I thought it would kill her.'

After another long pause, she said wearily, 'They are my family anyway. They're all I've got. Without my uncle we might have become the wives of village farmers or died young from malnutrition. So despite everything, I'm grateful to them for taking us in. I'm here because of them, and I will never forget that. Maybe I shouldn't be saying all these bad things about them – ' she stopped speaking abruptly, with that trademark look of alarm.

Vivian's face was oval, her nose and mouth were small, her eyes big, her eyebrows long and slender, her complexion dark and clear. As she sat silently looking at the floor, wondering if she'd told me too much, I thought: if you filled those eyes with laughter, ironed out the lines of worry on her forehead, the lines of a middle age that was arriving several years too soon, if you

163

chased away the fear which followed her about like a ghost, if you managed to repair the damage done by hardship, you would have a really pretty woman.

'Vivian,' I said gently, 'the only way to really get close to people is to get to know them, to get to know the things they've been through.'

'But you haven't told me anything about yourself.'

'I will. Are we in a hurry? This is going to be a long evening, and I hope there'll be many other long evenings, hundreds of them.'

'Men always make all kinds of promises,' she said.

I'm not making any to you, I wanted to say, but thought better of it. I sipped my beer, watched her confused, vulnerable face as she examined the plain dark brown rug on the floor.

At length I said, 'I think the important thing is that we all need friends in this place. This country is lonely.'

Vivian nodded, scanned my face and quickly looked away.

I steered the talk towards former romances. I talked briefly about Robo as though she were past tense (which indeed she was at the time, only I didn't know it). Vivian was stubbornly reticent and her past love life had to be coaxed out of her slowly and cunningly. As it came out I knew why she had been so reluctant to talk about it. Her first serious boyfriend was in Lagos, someone who lived in her neighbourhood in Coker, a chaotic, overpopulated area of horrible roads, no drainage and no sanitation, one more part of Lagos forgotten long ago by the powers that be. Seven years of going steady, though it was all very secret because her uncle and his wife would certainly have killed her if they'd found out. Then Vivian came out of nursing school with very good grades and got a good job in a high class private hospital in Apapa. The fellow started talking about marriage, they began to make plans. It was the happiest period of her life – she found her own place, was able, finally, to provide a home for her younger sister away from her uncle and his wife, even if it was only a room-and-parlour in insalubrious Okokomaiko, and she was about to get married. Her uncle's wife had taunted her all her life that no one would ever marry her and she had almost come to believe it, and now in only a few months she would prove her uncle's wife wrong, overturn that curse.

Then her fellow's behaviour inexplicably changed. He didn't turn up for days, when he did turn up, he was rude and temperamental. He implied there was a problem but didn't say what the problem was, and he soon stopped visiting. Weeks later she heard he was getting married to someone else, someone he had brought from his hometown fresh from school. Then she heard stories – he told people that she'd begun putting on airs because she now had a job, that Vivian was no longer humble enough to make a good wife. She, Vivian said, who was so humble she hated herself for it.

Trying to recover from that heartbreak, she took the popular option – joined a Pentecostal church where they cast out a variety of demons and saw your future spouse in visions, where the Lord took control of everything and all you had to do was pray very hard and fast occasionally. A well-built, foppish brother who was assistant pastor and who ran the singles' fellowship every Wednesday evening took an interest in her. She was flattered though the assistant pastor also seemed interested in quite a few other unmarried sisters. Then the assistant pastor, in brazen violation of the Holy Book, began to sleep with her – he promised marriage as soon as he had worked out a few financial problems he had. Vivian was confused but happy – they were committing sin, but the assistant pastor quoted the Bible so fluently you couldn't really doubt that he had good long-term intentions. Then, as the saying goes, the shit hit the fan. One Sunday, the head pastor veered away from the day's sermon and exposed the assistant pastor for what he was – an evil, wicked philanderer, a shepherd who was leading the flock under his care to damnation, a treasurer of souls who was dipping his fingers into the till, a vessel of the devil filled to the brim with carnal desire. Head pastor spoke of a long line of fornications, named names. Vivian, sitting in the front row with the other most zealous, heard her name being mentioned over the booming state-of-the-art loudspeakers and felt faint, thought she would die, that no one could recover from that kind of shame.

'This is the last chance for Brother Joseph, the assistant pastor, and the sisters he has led astray to come forward and confess their sins. This is the last chance!' head pastor thundered.

Vivian and the others (it turned out there were five of them) rushed forward. Brother Joseph fell flat on his face as soon as he got to his feet, his tears pouring into the plush carpet at the foot of the altar, writhing in contrition. Head pastor prayed mightily that the sinners be forgiven and asked the congregation to accept them back with open arms. But Vivian never went back to that church – the shame was too much.

It seemed to Vivian at that time that, as her uncle's wife had predicted, no man would ever marry her. When her uncle, whose respect for her had steadily grown as she effortlessly went through nursing school and had reached a crescendo when she got the job with that prestigious hospital, told her that one of the apprentices who had passed through his business was looking for a good wife and he'd thought of her, Vivian was grateful to him but was almost certain that something would go wrong. And she was right. Her would-be husband was loud and uncouth, a rural mind in the body of a savvy Lagos businessman, but she had accepted him. After what she'd been through she couldn't be too choosy, and anyway he seemed to have quite a bit of money. Then it turned out that his business was cocaine, and on one of his business trips his luck ran out at Bangkok airport. Vivian's uncle's wife said she had brought the poor man bad luck, he had gone and returned hundreds of times but just when he said he would marry her, he'd ended up in prison. Some people just carried misfortune around with them, Vivian's uncle's wife said, in fact some people's second name was ill luck. But Vivian didn't mourn for too long, for she had passed the American exam for foreign-trained nurses which was held in Ghana once a year. An agency in Lagos which was helping her process her papers sent word that she'd been offered a job in Washington DC. America would provide a fresh start, the past with its disappointments could be buried. But it hadn't turned out quite that way. There'd been another disappointment in Washington, something to do with a doctor who worked in the same hospital (which was why she'd started looking for another job as far away from DC as possible), but that wound was too fresh to be tampered with.

'Why am I telling you all this?' she asked suddenly, looking around wildly. She had a drowning look on her face, the wild horrified expression of someone who has lost grip and is bound for the bottom. The force of all that reawakened pain made her body tremble, the tears came slowly but steadily. 'Why am I telling you all these things about my life?' she sobbed.

It was distressing, but it was also an opening offered on a platter of gold. I swiftly crossed the distance between us on the long sofa and put my right arm around her neck and buried her face in my chest. She was too weak to resist, she clung to me helplessly, I made comforting noises while caressing her permed hair.

If my need for sex had not been so dire, I would simply have comforted the girl, led her to her bed, tucked her in and gone home. I'd taken advantage of women before, far more times than I cared to remember. I'd snatched at every opportunity to get some sex, but the scale of that girl's distress was so great it touched my conscience. At the same time my penis was rigid

167

against my jeans, and heavy on my mind were the ten months I'd gone without sex. Very fragile to start with, she'd been hit in four years with more disasters than most people encounter in a while lifetime. She needed genuine, reliable affection, and I knew I couldn't offer her that. All the affection I possessed had already been accounted for; I believed at the time that Robo was coming in a couple of months and there was no comparing the two of them. But I would find a nice way to handle things when the time came, I said to myself. I would try not to be too much of a bastard.

My ardour unimpaired by these thoughts, I set to work. I raised her fear-stricken face and kissed those drowning eyes, licking up the tears, running the tip of my tongue over her slender eyebrows. I traced the tearmarks with my tongue and when I reached her neck she fought me off and then pulled me close and garbled unintelligibly; when I nibbled at her neck, she seemed unable to breathe. It was obvious no one had given her this sort of treatment before. I lingered at her neck until she began to moan, began to declare, 'I'm going to die, I'm going to die,' her fingers locked around my neck like a hangman's rope. By the time I finished with her nipples, she had died and come back to life quite a few times; when I took off her panties, she was as flooded as a paddy field.

◆

The sex was voracious, energetic, adventurous, mind-blowing. My expectations after that Saturday afternoon at the Ezendus had been modest. Vivian looked incapable of anything more than prim sex, just a rung or two above masturbation. Instead I found a volcano that had lain dormant for several millennia. It appeared as though neither Vivian's first boyfriend who claimed she had begun putting on airs when she became a nurse in the high class Apapa hospital, nor Brother Joseph, assistant pastor and head of the singles' fellowship, nor the cocaine trader whose luck ran out in Bangkok, nor the DC doctor, had even scratched the surface of her sexuality. Every pore in her body gave off huge electric currents, and when I provided muff-eating service, her legs flew off the bed and fell back as violently as planes dropping out of the sky seconds after take-off, and I feared for my neck and my spinal cord.

Vivian's wild jack-knives, the screams that died in her throat as pleasure threatened to strangle her, her body's massive tremors and her gigantic orgasms excited me indescribably, my ego no doubt playing a large part. With ten months to make up for, I found within myself inexhaustible reservoirs of energy and a great deal of experimenting zeal. At first I saw Vivian once a week, on my one free day; she also arranged her shifts to keep that day free. Soon one day a week was no longer enough and we began to take advantage of whatever time came our way. On the days she finished work at five p.m., I would leave Oakland at four-thirty, take the I-580 to her place in Pleasanton, in twenty-five miles of traffic that was sometimes quite heavy, and we would go at each other until we were spent, dripping sweat and gasping for breath. Her alarm clock would wake me up at about nine-forty-five, I would take a quick bath, throw on my clothes and head for the warehouses, this time exiting from the I-580 at San Leandro to join the I-880. I plied that route so often I came to know every crack on the tarmac.

Pleasanton lived up to its name. It was a small town of well-kept, tree-lined streets and walkways and wide open spaces. The air around was fresh and plentiful. Though Vivian's room was in an enormous, barrack-like compound of two-storey apartment blocks, whose yellow and grey paint was beginning to fade, one of two such compounds at that end of Arroyo, you didn't get the feeling of being surrounded by large numbers of people. You rarely heard noises from the other apartments, and unlike in my part of Oakland, domestic quarrels never spilled out into the open. On weekend afternoons, Vivian and I would stroll down Arroyo to Bernal, past the leafy, stuccoed homes of the affluent, past the Pleasanton fairgrounds, to within sight of the I-680. We would sit on the grass for hours, facing a hill opposite the exit to Bernal, savouring the atmosphere, watching the huge articulated trucks roar past from the direction of San Jose. On the walk back it would be getting slightly chilly and Vivian would put an arm around my neck and glue her body to mine. The way people in the neighbourhood stared at us through their rearview mirrors and sometimes even stuck their necks out of their car windows made me feel like a trespasser, like someone strolling about at leisure in someone else's grounds, breathing someone else's air, and that feeling of wrong-doing made Pleasanton all the more enjoyable. It became my getaway place, where I could illicitly inhale the aroma of American middle-class success once or twice a week.

For Vivian I was a precious jewel that had materialised from fantasyland. Lying on her bed together watching the sitcoms, it was unlikely that she followed what was going on, for her eyes spent as much time staring at me as they did looking at the TV, probably trying to reassure herself that I was really there. If I turned and our eyes met, she would smile a little and reach across and stroke my forehead the way a child does and plant a soft kiss on my cheek or neck. She threw those three dangerous words – I love you – about like a lunatic playing with hand-grenades. She said them resolutely, defiantly, the way captured prisoners of war in the films state their names and the numbers of their units; no matter what you will do to me, she seemed to say, I love you; even if it will kill me, I love you.

A wonderful cook, she made Italian, Mexican, Moroccan and Thai dishes for me out of a heap of glossy cookbooks, searching the East Bay's farmers' markets and Oakland's Chinatown weekly for the freshest vegetables, fish and prawns. When I complimented her on her cooking, her eyes lit up like a flare and she became all silly and jaunty. She bought me a pair of garishly-coloured Nike trainers, the kind the newspapers say some black kids have killed for in the inner cities, Escape for Men by Calvin Klein, a wicked navy blue sweat-shirt and a bunch of Latin jazz CDs. Shamed, I bought her a fragrance by Van Cleef and Arpels and she quickly responded with a lovely check sports jacket.

Women have liked me a lot in the past, but I hadn't experienced anything approaching this. It scared me. How did you politely tell someone: Please don't buy me any more presents. I don't think I deserve all this devotion. I don't think any man, in fact anyone, should be worshipped like this. We humans are terribly unreliable creatures. Don't invest too much so that when the thing crumbles, as it's bound to, the pain won't kill you.

The talk somehow stumbled into marriage one day and Vivian declared, 'I love you so much I will do anything to have you for keeps, but if that's not possible I'll be grateful for whatever I can get.' But everything she did contradicted that claim. You didn't buy a man gifts worth, even with the best bargains, seven hundred dollars in six weeks and then meekly accept your fate the day he got up and walked away. No one was that self-sacrificing, that stupid. I was certain that deep inside her Vivian prayed fervently that this was the real thing, that the wonderful sex and the long walks would lead to marriage and so on and so forth, that the disappointments of her life and her loneliness in America would be conquered forever. Seeing as she had already been so deeply wounded four times in the past, what would become of her when that hope was crushed? It made me think of a drunken driver racing down a steep winding road at a hundred miles per hour.

I decided there was nothing I could do but allow time to sort things out. The sex was so good you had to be crazy to interfere with the flow. I tried to be as nice as possible. I successfully hid my irritation as the hundreds of kisses landed on my forehead, my cheek, my neck. I smiled nicely when Vivian planted herself without warning on my lap, smiled nicely, too, at the unceasing I love yous.

When Vivian wasn't cooking for me or giving me presents or making love to me, she sat at her little desk beside her dressing table and wrote letters home. She would hold her head up with her left hand and cover pages and pages of ruled light blue paper with her careful writing that leaned slightly to the left, occasionally darting glances at me lying on the bed reading a novel. The letters to Isioma, her sister in Nigeria, were usually thick, like university term papers. She related every detail of her life in America and gave precise instructions on how the money she sent with every letter would be dispensed.

'. . . Use hundred and fifty dollars to pay your part of the rent and keep three hundred dollars for your other needs. Use fifty dollars to pay for Uju's extra lessons. You know Auntie is a greedy woman, please don't give the money for Uju's extra lessons to her, give the money to Uncle himself. Tell him that I don't think the money they are charging is too much. It is very important that Uju should pass her SSSC exams this time and I will send some more money next month for the additional books.

'I'm glad you liked the shoes and bags I sent. I'm not surprised that Auntie grumbled as usual. I haven't forgotten how wicked she was to us, and I know that in her heart she still doesn't wish us well, but please let's continue doing our best for her. She is still a member of our family, whether we like it or not.

172

'I'm sorry to hear that Uncle's business has not yet improved in spite of all the money I have sent him. Please tell him that I have some pressing needs right now, and I won't be able to send anything to him now, but as soon as things are better for me, I will send whatever I can.'

Vivian was forever searching for people travelling to Nigeria to send things through, was always at the San Jose flea market looking for the right size of tennis shoes for a cousin or the right colour of shoe and bag for a friend. Her sister's replies to her letters read like ledgers:

'. . . I changed the money at N82 to one dollar at Federal Palace. I gave Uncle N3000 to pay for Uju's lessons. Uncle said Nnamdi needed a new pair of glasses and I gave him N1000 for the glasses. Uncle was complaining that things are so bad for him that he has not paid the town union dues and they say they will expel him from the meeting so I gave him N1000 to clear his dues. I paid N7,500 for my part of the rent, I used N800 to change the curtains in my room. They were getting so old . . .'

But the needs kept growing. Her uncle wrote:

'I am too sad to inform you that no progress yet on the case of the boys who duped me all my money. We report to the police station more than fifty time but up to now the police continue to do us come today come tomorrow. I think the police have collected money from the boys. One of our towns boy who travel to Belgium want to help me money is the only problem. He can give me share in one container with another of our towns boy. The amount of my own part is N500,000. I know it is a big amount but

173

anything you can do God will bless you more and more. My dearest daughter you and Jesus Christ are my only hope in this world.'

'It's good to help your people back home,' I said to Vivian, 'but you have to remember you can't solve all their problems. Don't stretch yourself too much.'

'I know. But there's so much suffering and I'm trying to do my best. I'm the only one they have.'

'There's always been suffering in this world and there probably always will be. Your sister is your only real responsibility. Your uncle and his family, if I remember correctly, weren't exactly very loving when you were growing up.'

'But it doesn't mean I can't help them,' Vivian said. 'Darling, I know you are thinking of my best interests, but this money I make really doesn't mean anything to me if it is not being used to help my people.'

'All I'm saying is don't overdo it.'

The strain sometimes showed. She would be at her desk writing a letter and on her face would be all those lines of weariness. She would look for a little while like an old lady tired of the world, who's about to finally give up. But if she noticed I was looking, she'd force herself to brighten up and give me a quick little smile.

My only interest when I first met Vivian had been sexual, but as time passed I began to develop some affection for her, though nothing near the intensity of her love for me. Her generosity to her people in Nigeria seemed excessive (the only money I'd sent home was a hundred dollars for my younger sister, Nwaka), even foolish, but at the same time her willingness to sacrifice so much to help people who'd made her childhood very miserable was almost saintly. Vivian's reckless love for me frightened me, and the fact that she hadn't learnt to protect herself after so many previous heartbreaks was surely moronic, yet I sometimes thought of that stark vulnerability as a special kind of honesty.

◆

I turned twenty-nine on 18 July. Vivian took me out to Skates, a restaurant on the Berkeley Marina. She wore a short, tight orange dress, big earrings and bangles and fashionable black platform shoes, and I'd never seen her so radiant. She'd reserved a good seat at the far end of the restaurant, so close to the glass wall you felt you were in the middle of the Bay which stretched out on all sides, dark and quietly busy in places, loud with light and colour in others. The restaurant was packed and noisy. A birthday party was going on at the table next to ours. Apart from a thin young man and a young woman in rimless glasses who was probably his wife, the other twelve or so people in the party looked about seventy, but they were having a wild time, laughing, singing and shouting. A father and mother across the room were struggling to keep their three little children under control. The kids were fighting and crying and spilling the soup and searching for things under the table and shifting their seats and the table about. The waitresses, infected, it seemed, with the mood of the place, waltzed between the tables and appeared to be quite careless with the trays, but nothing fell.

Vivian asked me to choose a wine. Not being of the drinking-wine-in-restaurant class, I said the first thing that came to my mind, 'Piper Sonoma'.

'How can we drink California wine on your birthday for God's sake?' Vivian said, her eyes narrowing in mock amazement, looking more relaxed, more confident that I'd ever seen her. 'Let's have a Dom Perignon, please,' she said.

'You can't fail with that,' the big-boned waitress said with a wink.

The sea bass was excellent. 'Nearly as good as your cooking,' I told Vivian, and she smiled broadly and leaned across the table to kiss my forehead. We talked about the future. I said I wanted to go back to school for an MBA or a masters in information technology as soon as I could. I hoped I would be able to save enough money in a year or two. It was the kind of night when your head filled with hope, when nothing seemed impossible or even particularly difficult. Vivian said she hoped her sister, who'd come out of university with a good degree in law and was doing national service, would get an American visa when she finished early in the coming year.

Vivian's birthday gift to me was a Rolex, a big complicated thing with four different dials, the kind of watch advertised by mountain climbers and underwater explorers and people like that. It must have cost a fortune, and deeply moved, I leaned over and gave her a kiss on the lips. It was the first time I'd ever done anything like that, and it took her a long while to recover from the shock.

'You know I really love you, Obi,' she said, her eyes misting over. 'I know you don't believe in such things, but I really do love you.'

I nodded and smiled sweetly and reached out and covered her left hand with mine and squeezed. She wiped her eyes with her other hand and stared at my face.

'I'm sorry,' she said.

'What about?'

'The way I am. I'm too emotional; I should learn to control myself.'

'Don't talk nonsense, Vivian. The problem with the world is that there are not enough emotional people around these days. That's why people are so much like pieces of wood or calculators, always checking profit and loss in everything. To be genuinely emotional in today's world is wonderful. I admire you, and I like you very much.'

That was another first coming from me and Vivian's misty eyes became confused, as if she wasn't sure any more who was sitting in front of her. I too was surprised at my own generosity. The way the relationship had worked was that Vivian did all the giving and my own role was just to receive graciously. My new mood probably came from sitting in that charming restaurant, surrounded by the Bay, enchanted by the lights of San Francisco, from the excellent bass and the hot seafood chowder that came before it and the Dom Perignon; from Vivian's bright orange dress and her hopeful happy face, from those ten months I'd spent before I met her in which I'd sometimes been scared that loneliness and sexual starvation would kill me; from a deep sense of gratitude.

'Obi darling, do you really mean that?'

'Of course, I mean *that*. You are a wonderful person. Your problem is that you've allowed people, lousy people at that, to make you think you're not. You must never let that happen ever again.'

Vivian nodded, and stared at my fingers stretched out on the table covering hers.

I didn't know as I sat there, smiling and trying to get her to look up, surrounded by the high-volume chattering and laughing of the sated and slightly drunk, that in only a matter of days I would hurt her as deeply as anyone ever had.

We left the restaurant a little before midnight. It was such a happy night I didn't think we should go home just yet. I suggested we check out an Ethiopian-owned jazz bar in San Francisco called Rosselas, which I'd read about in a newspaper. Even when I'd just bought my car and was excitedly exploring the Bay Area, I'd avoided San Francisco because it appeared to

177

me too large and dangerous – a place where you were sure to get lost even with a map, or get into police trouble. But that night I was in the mood to try anything.

I drove Vivian's late-model green hatchback Mazda, with shiny black upholstery, while she navigated, a map of the city spread out on her lap. Her head was leaning on my shoulder, her hand stroking my neck. The wine in my head mixed with the cool air pouring in through the car windows and the heavy thumping of Notorious B.I.G. and Brandy's caressy singing on 107.7 FM made me very buoyant. I was driving too fast, and only came to my senses after I nearly ran into a car in front of me that braked quickly at a traffic light. Even at that time of night traffic was heavy, especially at the toll gates just before Oakland Bridge. As you approached the clusters of cleverly lit skyscrapers, San Francisco made Oakland look like a down-on-his-luck cousin, but the streets were ordinary-looking. The people, half of whom seemed to be tramps, didn't match the grandeur of the tall buildings. Van Ness was filled with speeding cars that stopped abruptly at each of the traffic lights which lined the street like a column of guards, and then sped off again, as though they were in a race; the pavements were thronged with people. A group of youths were playing basketball in a floodlit court and there were quite a few joggers about. The bar was at California by Divisidaro. We missed the turning to California the first time, and had to drive a long distance, past several more traffic lights, to make a U-turn. We found the bar but then spent the next ten minutes looking for a place to park, and finally found one outside a large dark church that looked like it had been built in the twelfth century.

Rosselas was packed, lively and warm. The audience was a mixture of black and white and yellow of various ages. All the seats were taken so Vivian and I leaned against a wall. The singer, a black woman approaching middle age but bursting with energy, her ample body viciously clamped in a tiny black dress, had the crowd belting out the choruses as she ran through a string of standards.

> I just called to say I love you
> I just called to say I love you
> I just called to say I love you
> And to tell you how much I care

> What's love got to do
> Got to do with it
> What's love but a second-hand emotion

I drank beer and became even happier. I wrapped my arms around Vivian and she wrapped hers around me. A traffic jam of I-love-yous, I-will-forever-love-yous and I-will-always-love-yous built up in her throat. We rubbed against each other gently, deliberately fiercening hungers which we would fully satisfy later. It didn't seem impossible as the night progressed and I put away more beer and the singing got even livelier that I could grow to love Vivian very much, nearly as much as she said she loved me.

The band switched to jazz. A tall light brown guy, in a dark flowered shirt buttoned up to his neck, blew fantastic hopes and dreams out of his sax. The music invaded your body, made your stomach very warm, made your legs shake of their own accord. You felt a huge burst of energy as the sax soared and the music turned into a wild uncontrollable thing. You wanted to holler, you wanted to fly, you wanted to fuck, you wanted to sing. Then the music became playful, the sax player tossed tantalising notes at you, now sharp and short, now incredibly drawn out, now jagged and unfriendly. After a while he seemed trapped in his own dexterity, to have turned his back forever on his audience. Then he began to rise again, to be possessed once more by that unstoppable madness, and then out of nowhere he brought you back to earth, his notes long and sad, and you remembered things – like that Vivian and I were having a great evening, but that Robo would soon be here and how on earth was I going to handle that situation so this wonderful girl didn't get hurt very badly yet again; like that it was all very well to go out to a good restaurant and eat excellent seafood and drink champagne and feel like a full member of the affluent society, but my dreary job at the warehouses waited for me later that day; like that I hadn't seen my parents and my sisters in almost a year and didn't know when next I would.

And when the sax player began to climb again, I couldn't go with him. My arms were wrapped round the sweet, shapely woman by my side and her arms were wrapped round me, but the saxophone had stolen something from me, had led a crowd of fears and frustrations past the delicious headiness of that evening, and I was probably already in the grip of a premonition that disaster lay just round the corner.

Nebraska Man

Disaster struck the week after, in the shape of a letter from Nigeria delivered by DHL. I wasn't expecting urgent mail from home and the first, wild thought that came to my mind was that my parents and my sisters, who'd called to wish me a happy birthday three days before, had been wiped out in a car accident. The letter, from Robo, was almost as devastating as the news of my family's violent extinction would have been.

'. . . I'm sorry to write you this kind of letter so close to your birthday, but believe me, Obi, I think it will be even

more unfair to keep putting it off. Since you left for
America I have thought about us a lot and I think it will be
better for the two of us to end this relationship. Being in a
relationship where the other person is so far away has been
very difficult for me. I missed you so much after you left
that I fell ill. I have tried very hard to cope, God knows
how hard I've tried, but it's just too much for me.

'I still care about you very much but it's just impossible to
continue like this. I will always remember you fondly and I
really, really wish you the best . . .'

There was a story my mother told often, of how on the day in
1970 my father bought our first TV, a small black-and-white
affair with elaborately worked gold-coloured knobs, my elder
sister, Adaku, and I had sat on the floor right next to it, trying
to figure out how to touch the people inside it. Then in the
middle of a documentary about construction work, an enormous
rock hill was pulverised by dynamite, and Adaku and I had
screamed and run crying from the living room, our excitement
replaced by cyclonic terror. It had been a long while before we
were persuaded to come near the unpredictable TV again.
Remembering now the way my heart exploded when I was halfway through Robo's letter, I think of that rock hill that was torn
to pieces by dynamite. The blood drummed in my head. I
experienced a massive disorientation, like a man who goes to
sleep on his bed and wakes up in the middle of hell. Struggling
to retain a grip on the world, I crept like a thief over the letter,
taking the words one after the other, reassembling the sentences
as though the sheet of paper had been shredded and had to be
put back together again: *God . . . knows . . . how . . . hard . . . I
. . . tried . . .*, beginning the arguments with those words which
would rage for weeks inside my head like a grassland fire in

181

harmattan. *Of course, you tried, of course you were supposed to try and to keep trying. The long slow afternoons in my room in our house at Yaba, lying naked while jazz flowed all around us and it felt like we were swimming in music. You didn't mind David Sanborn, Grover Washington, people like that, but you said Miles and Coltrane required too much work to follow, were too deep, you said all those hours and hours listening to instrumentals made you think too much, made you moody. You wanted something jaunty, a popular song that you could sing along with, Janet or Whitney, you called them like they were your schoolfriends, or you wanted Fela, you wanted to dance naked, to shake your waist small-small, and we argued about music, laughing, our bodies still sweating from recent lovemaking, touching all the time in all kinds of places. Of course, you had to try, that was what we had been building all those moments for, so you would try and keep trying. Otherwise, what was all that for? Why did we give each other fourteen years of our lives? When in my cramped room at the university we had to stifle our love-making noises because we knew bastards like Bronzo and the Hook had their ears glued to the door listening for the slightest sounds about which they would tease us later, and it somehow made the love-making all the more exciting. It all had to add up to something. And how can you now say you can't continue, how is it possible that you can't continue? Does it mean that you've been conning me all this time because if what has gone before was genuine, then there's no way you could just break it up? Because it really did amount to a whole lot. It was my entire life, our fucking lives left in each other's care. So how do you throw it away like dirty water? After I've waited for you for one year? When did you decide you couldn't continue? Even when inside Vivian my thoughts were of you. Of course there is no comparison. Why didn't I feel guilty about sleeping with Vivian? And my other infidelities? You know how it is, the flesh is weak and all that. And anyway, after almost one year of wanking off in America, no one would blame me. Anyway, there has never been any question of who really mattered; you, of course, you a thousand times over, you only.*

I dialled Robo's number. It was about noon, about three a.m. in Nigeria, but I didn't care what time it was. I didn't care if Robo's sour-faced father came to the phone and abused me thoroughly. I didn't care. I dialled several times but the call didn't go through, then the next time I dialled a recorded female voice came on – *All trunks lines are busy, please try later.* That response to an international call must be unique to my wretched country, I thought bitterly. I didn't know a lot about how telephone systems worked, but I couldn't understand how any part of the globe, even the poorest of the poor, the least developed country in the world by all indices, would have difficulty in connecting a call that had been made from thousands of miles away, how a country would be so inefficient that all its 'trunks' would be busy. I hated my country that afternoon more than I've ever hated it; more, I'm sure, than I would ever hate it again. What kind of incompetent godforsaken place was that? It was impossible to call *from* Nigeria, and now it was impossible to make a call *to* Nigeria, lousy big-for-nothing hole, land of loudmouths and incompetents, of rogues and barbarians. All lines were still busy about half an hour later, and were still busy an hour later.

Meanwhile, the argument with Robo's letter was unabating. *When we went on holiday to the UK in 1992, you were so excited at the prospect of seeing your eldest brother, Justin, who lectured at Reading. You'd received cards from him on your birthdays, cards that always somehow arrived on the day or a day or two earlier even though the mail in Nigeria was so erratic. And your whole family received his big Christmas cards with snowmen and pine and all that and he sometimes called at*

Christmas or on New Year's Day, but he hadn't come home for fifteen years and his phone was almost always disconnected because he was forever working on all those terribly important articles for extremely academic journals, so it was impossible to get in touch with him, but you had his address and you wanted to surprise him. So we caught a train from Ealing Broadway or a place with a name like that. And at the station in Reading we were surprised that many of the people we spoke to didn't know how we could get to the university. Are these English people daft or are they just being nasty, we wondered. Then we found a cab rank near the station, and at the back of the black cab I noticed you were nervous, maybe wondering if it was such a good idea to go and see him without warning, maybe while walking around the station trying to find out how to get to the university, your enthusiasm had begun to wane. After all Justin hadn't been home in such a long time, he would virtually be a stranger. And then we found his little redbrick house off a street of sturdy trees and wild flowers as quiet as death except for one red car which tore down the road as though it were a race track and disappeared round a bend. Justin's sallow sad eyes of a terminally ill man who had stared for months at the roof from his hospital bed, his old brown sweater which had a damp smell, the three disparate old seats in his living room, no doubt from separate garage sales, his extremely cold, threatened voice, his crushingly English manners, the offer of tea thrown at us in a way that made it clear it wasn't meant to be accepted, the pretty nervous white girl who greeted us too brightly, introduced curtly as 'my friend Tara', the way Tara, in her own nondescript sweater and too-tight, jump-up jeans, had tried to cancel out the attractiveness of her features, her unkempt yellow hair hanging on her head like a frayed rag, her face smudged at the corners with what looked like dirt and made me think of Oliver Twist, her cracked fingernails like a labourer's, and the tomes of books, all about

Africa, taking up all the space in the small living room, ironic for that couple who were as unAfrican as Greenland; confronted with all these and with the foolishness of your quest to surprise that man who had worked very hard to eliminate the possibility of surprise from his life, who had painstakingly built that crypt of books and English manners, you, usually such a strong person, cried all the way back to London. And I held you and rocked you, as the eyes of the people in the compartment pretended to be locked forever to the paperbacks they were clutching. Your hands were around me and you shook and sniffed on that slow train, which moved like something from colonial Nigeria. I tried to explain to you that Justin wasn't just being wicked or anything like that, but had had to construct a new life in that place all alone and it couldn't have been easy. What I didn't know at the time was that I would also have to deal with a loneliness of the type that had turned Justin into an Englishman in an old brown sweater among tomes on African anthropology and the village hierarchies of Kalahari Bushmen. For one year the most precious thing I had was the hope that you were coming over to join me. With you I would cheat the loneliness of this place, I would never become a prematurely old man in an old brown sweater with a damp smell. What am I supposed to do now? When people have shared what we've shared, don't they become inseparable?

I finally got through by phone three hours after I'd started trying, but no one answered. I kept trying and the phone just rang and rang and then was cut off. I wasn't sure who to blame this time. They had no way of knowing I was the one calling, or had they? Had they travelled to their hometown as they did from time to time? I lay on my bed, dying of frustration. *Before I left for America we had virtually become man and wife. Our rough times were behind us. The time I slept with your friend Cash-ewnut (I forget now why you all called her that name), and you*

185

got so mad at me you didn't talk to me for eight months, during which time you went out with Folarin. That hurt terribly, first because you went out with someone at all, then because it was Folarin, Mr God's Gift to the Nigerian Woman, arrogant, dressy bastard, with a brain so tiny it wouldn't show up under the most powerful microscope in the world. That was an insult, but I did nothing all those months but work to get you back. I sent our friends to you, I wrote you stupid letters and verses, I persevered, I endured every imaginable humiliation. And one day you just couldn't stand that bastard any more, and we got back together again. You know many Nigerian men would never have been able to live it down, having to go flat on their belly to beg a woman to take them back. But I did it for eight months and I never brought it up again except as a joke. I did it because you meant so much to me. After that I still had the occasional affair, but I was much more discreet. I had learnt the hard way to respect you. The last few months before I left we were together nearly twenty-four hours every day. At parties we sat in a corner, holding each other, even though it was bad form for a guy to come to a party and sit in a corner with his girlfriend. But form had ceased to matter. People might say it was because BTF had crumbled and I was no longer quite such a hot yuppie and was holding on to what I had left. But you know it went beyond that. What we had had become so deep and wonderful. Adversity had strengthened it until we were closer than most husbands and wives ever get. How can you cast it aside just like that? How can you?

Those feverish pleas addressed to a sheet of cream writing paper lasted all day, interrupted by desperate, unsuccessful, attempts to get through to Robo's house by phone. When the public execution of alleged armed robbers by firing squad was one of Nigeria's most popular forms of entertainment, the aspect I had always found intriguing was the way the men who were being led to their deaths continued to protest their innocence. It was clearly hopeless, you would think the sensible thing to do would be to conserve whatever energy they had left to face death with. But no, the arguments went on and on while they were bound to the stakes, some kept shouting their innocence while the soldiers took aim and the crowds who had ringside seats and those who watched at home on TV held their breath. Some continued protesting even as the bullets cut their bodies open like beef. My appeals to Robo's letter were like those dying armed robbers' pleas of innocence. Her letter was unequivocal, it didn't give room for hope, and anyway it was just a lifeless sheet of paper, but I argued tirelessly, dredging up incidents, places, moods from memory to support my hopeless cause.

I was still there at eleven p.m., lying on my bed, clutching the phone to my chest the way you clutch a hot water bottle. It was time to leave for my shift at the warehouses but I didn't move from the bed. Though I'd almost earned two weeks' wages, I decided there and then that I would never return to that job. I freed myself of that dreary place and my depressing partners on the night shift just like that. Very few things mattered at that time. Robo's letter had set me free, as free as a lunatic or a dead man. David Letterman, usually one of my favourite Americans, came on TV, but he wasn't funny at all that night. He was just a stupid man with a funny face who recycled silly jokes like garbage.

◆

Over the next two weeks I continued to enact the great drama of my heartbreak. The stage was my narrow room of secondhand furniture. I was sole actor and most of the monologue took place inside my head. Now and again I couldn't keep it in and began to address my pain to the room until I caught myself and, scared

I was going mad, pulled the words that were about to spill out back inside. My props were my telephone, also secondhand, and a steadily increasing litter of Heineken cans and Kentucky Fried Chicken cartons, for though I was so terribly wounded that I shouldn't have cared about food and such mundane things, the demons in my stomach had no respect for heartbreak and every afternoon I slunk out of my room, famished, and walked to KFC on Grand Avenue to buy greasy chicken, fries and coleslaw.

Heartlessly, the world outside my room, luxuriating in summer sunshine, took no notice of my pain. The Seven Eleven across the road on Grand was full of young people in little T-shirts and shorts, and even a few naked, hairy chests, lugging cartons of beer to their cars; they called out to friends driving past in traffic, their monstrous loudspeakers pounding the street with defiant music rather like an artillery bombardment. Further up the road a good-natured crowd watched some men playing chess outside an antique shop. The small Italian restaurant beside the antique shop was even fuller than usual. All around Lake Merritt people were strolling, jogging, sitting on the grass, leaning out of parked cars, eating out of brown bags, shouting greetings at passing cars; it was like a mammoth picnic. Lovely women in skimpy exercise wear and big trainers strode smartly out of a gym above the Vietnamese laundry, brushed past me, said 'excuse me' with wicked smiles, ducked into their sleek new cars, and slid into the heavy traffic. Through the glass front of Madrid's you saw more lovely women, their hair thick and drippy with shampoo, browsing through *Essence*, their mouths wide open in exclamations you couldn't hear, and above their heads were long shelves of relaxers and suchlike which did miraculous things to black hair.

My voice as I gave my order at KFC often sounded to me like a stranger's: weak and confused. On the walk back to my room I kept bumping into people because my head was filled with pleas in response to Robo's letter. *The first time I spoke to you, it was the bravest act of my life. That day we freshers were all waiting to register, and because of the usual incompetence – someone had locked away the registration forms in a safe and was nowhere to be found or they had run out of forms or something like that – they had left us baking in the sun for hours. Everyone was wearing jeans as if it was the university's uniform – stretch jeans, pre-faded, tapered, ribbed, all kinds – wandering around the lawn, sitting on benches or on the grass. Bronzo put me up to it – he said you were looking at me with a lot of interest and that I should go up and talk to you. I knew it was a lie, but I felt unusually brave that morning, maybe because it was my first day at university, the beginning of a new phase and all that. I didn't even know where I found that voice which said with false cool, 'I don't think these people are ever going to get themselves organised, why don't you come and have a drink with my friend and me?' You sized me up and you seemed about to say no then changed your mind. I remember you were wearing a big white shirt over faded jeans. Many of the other girls wore tight tops, but maybe because you knew you didn't have any hefty breasts to emphasise, you opted for something roomy. There was a wind as we walked to the kiosk across the road and your shirt filled up like a balloon. Bronzo walked behind us, kicking himself for not having asked you himself. My hands shook like hell as I brought your Coke to the table, and I placed the bottle so clumsily I spilled some of it on the table and on your lap. I was so full of shame and apology, but you said it was nothing at all. You brought out a flowered handkerchief and cleaned the table and your trousers, and that seemed to set the tone for our relationship. I was always blundering and messing things up and you always cleaned up the mess. When you started dating Folarin, it taught me how valuable you really were when I had begun to take you for granted. America has taught me that even more emphatically. So how can you leave me now? Now, when I have finally learnt your true value? How can you leave me now?*

From invoking memories in support of my cause, I moved on to hating myself for the crime of denial and cowardice, i.e. I knew it was going to happen but had refused to acknowledge the fact because I couldn't bear to face the consequences. The very first phonecall I made to Robo when I got to America, when in an anguished voice she'd asked me, *Why did you have to go and leave me alone?*, had warned me that we were at the beginning of the end. She had gone on to apologise for being soppy and for adding to the things I had to bother about instead of making my burden lighter. However, I had known she meant it when she asked that question but had suppressed the knowledge, preferring to keep on deluding myself. The texture of conversation when I called her had changed over time – more talk about who was going out with who, what was happening in Lagos, etc. but hardly any talk about ourselves. It was, of course, still full of laughter, but we'd begun to sound more like good friends than lovers. *You knew she was slipping away, you knew there was nothing you could do about it, but lousy coward that you are, you concealed the knowledge from yourself. You needed to go on believing in that wonderful love back home, matured over time like wine, which you were going to import into America. You needed a counter to the long nights in the desolate guards' room of the warehouses, to the emptiness of your life, so you began to deceive yourself. Even when Robo's mother said on the phone that she was away on suspiciously long audits in distant corners of Nigeria and you didn't speak to her for weeks, you still refused to get the message. You waited patiently for the next opportunity to call, pretending you believed her mother, when you knew that Robo's father would never send his daughter to such faraway places when he had a bunch of young sufferhead employees in the firm. You knew all along it was*

190

over, but you lied to yourself. And now you are still lying, pretending you've been shocked, shattered, devastated, etc., feasting on contrived pain and self-pity.

Why did you think Robo would leave her life in Nigeria for you? – her family, the accountancy firm which she'll inherit from her father, in which she's already deputy managing partner after only three years; all her friends, the wonderful life of one of a small, spoilt élite in a land of poverty and suffering, as in the old Wole Soyinka poem, the one-eyed kings – and queens and princes and princesses – in the land of the blind; all that for you and the uncertainty of America? BTF collapsed, you lost your job, your future vanished, hers didn't. Don't you think she knows that? What do you have to offer her? – this room with a yellowed bath and rusted taps, your creaky Toyota Corolla in exchange for their house with two living rooms, six bedrooms, six bathrooms and ten air-conditioners in Gbagada, where the air-conditioners hum twenty-four hours a day whether or not there is a cut in the public power supply, her father's Mercedes Benzes, her own sexy Golf? Of course, you knew she wasn't going to come, how could you not have known that it was over the moment you got on that plane? Of course you knew, but your need for self-delusion was so great you had to stage a one-year waiting-for-Robo charade. You stupid fool, you spent hundreds of dollars on phone bills, you bought an expensive TV and subscribed to the most expensive cable package available so Robo would have variety when she got here. You collected all the summer programmes and flyers in the Bay Area – Shakespeare-in-the-park in Oakland, Walnut Creek and San Ramon, street music festivals and food and craft fairs in San Francisco and Berkeley, bargain trips to Yerba Buena and Alcatraz, the grandest wine fields in Napa Valley, the best restaurants in Monterey, Jelly's Last Jam at the Golden Gate – it was going to be a magical summer, the sun smiling overhead, your love once again by your side, planning a wonderful future together in America, a new life in the land of plenty . . . You pathetic fool!

Vivian, who had all but been forgotten as I acted out the tragedy of my heartbreak, called me one morning during the self-hating phase of my drama. What had become of me? She'd expected me the day before when her shift ended at 5.00 p.m., but I hadn't shown up and hadn't called; was anything the matter? Considering how much bitterness was in my head at that time, my answer wasn't too bad.

'Vivian,' I said, 'I have some personal problems I need to work out, I'll call you when I'm feeling better.' I repeat, my response wasn't bad considering my condition, but I put the receiver down as soon as I had finished speaking, and Vivian called me back immediately. Perhaps if I hadn't put the receiver down so abruptly, things would have turned out differently. In the event when she called the second time Vivian had begun to sound like a nervous wreck, an incredible transformation from the normal girl of the first call.

'What is the matter, Obi, darling? Why did you hang up on me? Please, have I offended you?' and so on and so forth. Again, considering that I was so bitter at the time and that in addition I was getting very irritated at all that uncalled-for nervousness, which reminded me of the Vivian I'd met at the Ezendus' in May – the frightened, characterless girl whose face was filled with lines of premature middle age whom I'd only taken an interest in because of my desperate need for sex – considering all that, I remained quite civil.

'Vivian,' I said, 'you haven't done anything to me. I'm just a bit depressed. I'll call you as soon as I feel better,' and I put the receiver down. And the phone rang yet again, and hearing her blurt out the same questions in a voice that had deteriorated even further, I cruelly put the receiver down and then took it off the hook. I lay back on my bed, the phone still clutched to my chest like a hot water bottle, and returned to my drama of heartbreak.

I don't know how Vivian found my apartment block. I'm positive I never gave her the address; I'd made it clear from the beginning that our meeting place would be her house. Mine was out of bounds. The sound of the buzzer three hours later woke me from sleep (in spite of the magnitude of my heartbreak, I still dozed off occasionally). Vivian's voice on the intercom, as she pleaded with me to let her come up to my room, sounded like the whining of a wounded puppy, 'Please, you have to tell me what is wrong. Please, Obi, don't do this to me, I'm begging you. Please tell me what I have done . . .'

My answer, I recall now with a lot of shame and regret (I swear I wasn't myself, the way Vivian was demeaning herself made something snap in my head), my answer, delivered in my coldest voice, was: 'Stop bothering me, don't call my number ever again, and if you ever come here again, I'll turn you over to the police.'

Several days later I got through to Robo's house and her father answered. His voice startled me for I'd given up hope of ever speaking to anyone in the house; I'd kept dialling the number merely as part of the ritual of heartbreak.

'It's Obi,' I said, 'from America. I'd like to speak to Robo, please.'

'Obi,' he said, 'how are you doing?' His tone of voice was unbelievably gentle.

'I'm fine, sir.'

'Obi, Robo is not here.'

'Is she travelling?'

'No,' he said and paused. 'She didn't travel. Well, as a matter of fact, well, she's in fact in her husband's place.'

'I see,' I said very quietly, and put the phone down on the floor beside the bed. There was a second massive explosion in my chest, but now I see that it was also the beginning of my recovery. Fresh bitterness rose inside me like vomit. I called Robo a treacherous slut on whom I'd wasted my affection. I called myself a fool, an imbecile, a moron, a coward, a dreamer, a blind bastard, a bloody romantic, a despicable failure. I blamed Nigeria: if it wasn't such a screwed-up place I wouldn't have left and this wouldn't have happened. I blamed my parents and my friends: how could Robo be getting married and no one had mentioned it? It was impossible that no one had heard, there must have been a conspiracy. I even blamed AT & T: if their fucking phone bills hadn't been so high, I would have spoken to Robo more often than I did and that would have saved our relationship. I spent hours and hours hunting for people to blame, to hate. But the drama of heartbreak soon came to an end. It had reached its climax the moment Robo's father said she was in her husband's place and I said 'I see'. All that came after was fluff, and after I'd hated and blamed everything I could find, there were no more lines left for me to say. I soon became sick of the stink of stale beer and frying oil that had taken over my room. I didn't need anyone to tell me that it was now time to get on with my life.

◆

When I was at university, Nebraska Man had been as permanent a fixture of a bar close to our house in Yaba as the bar's ancient dirt-blackened stools. He was a tall man with black curly hair and an overripe-orange complexion which gave rise to a wide variety of rumours about his origins – some said his father was Nigerian and his mother mixed-race American; some said his mother was Red Indian, his father Sierra Leonean; the malicious said he had been born in a whorehouse in New York and his father could have been any of about five hundred men. The fact

194

that he resolutely refused to comment on those rumours encouraged people with vivid imaginations to concoct even wilder versions. Seated on a tall barstool, Nebraska Man would, once his audience ensured a steady supply of Gulder, go on and on in a gently flowing American accent about his adventures in God's Own Country. His stories always began with: 'When I was in Nebraska – ', 'When I was in Houston – ', 'When I was in LA – '. He became Nebraska Man probably because Nebraska sounded to his listeners more exotic, more fantasyland-like than the other places he said he'd been to. Nebraska Man had been a firefighter, swinging from helicopters to put out end-of-the-world blazes in fifty-storey buildings. He had also fought 'gooks' in Vietnam, he'd done odd jobs for the Mafia, and he'd been part of a dirty politician's campaign for governor. In short, Nebraska Man had done everything his beer-ruled brain could grasp at to excite his crowd of fans – university students, young office workers and the unemployed, who all had their dreams of America.

Over time, Nebraska Man graduated from Gulder to cocaine, and to finance his habit he began to haunt Lagos's busiest streets, spinning yarns about how he had just come in from America and someone had stolen his wallet and how he needed to catch a taxi to the American embassy and just needed 'a few nairas'. For many Lagosians, a genuine American accent is an overpowering thing, and Nebraska Man was very successful at first, but all good things come to an end, and after a while nearly everyone had heard about his stolen wallet and his need to get to the American embassy. Wafer-thin and as filthy as a rubbish-dump rat, by the time I moved to America Nebraska Man walked the streets at all times of day and night, his mind in shreds, waiting for death.

He walked into my dreams when I was coming out of my drama of heartbreak. He walked in the rain, shivering, holding his rags to his body, dirty water squishing out of his torn brown shoes as though they were rotten oranges. He didn't need to say a word, his mere presence was enough. He stood for what happened to you when you failed abroad and returned home in shame. He was the road that could not be taken. Nebraska Man wordlessly told me I had to somehow find the energy to succeed in America, that failure was unthinkable. I had to stop rolling about in the vomit of self-pity, had to give up all the sense of injury I had hoarded like contraband gemstones. I had to get a green card somehow and find a better job than being a security guard. I had to save some money and go to graduate school. I had to begin sending money home to my people. It wasn't going to be easy starting life all over again at twenty-nine, but it had to be done, there was no alternative. And while I slaved for material success I had to guard my ability to laugh at myself and the world, for a success earned at the expense of a sense of humour wasn't success at all. I also had to find a locker for memory, for Robo and the sounds and smells of Lagos and the glorious days in BTF and all that, a locker from which I could take out what I wanted now and again and thereafter put it back. The past was an important part of me, but it had to be restrained so the present could breathe.

America was all around me, immense, indifferent, frightening, but also incredibly varied, challenging and, in spite of large corporations who were sacking thousands of people to please Wall Street, still full of opportunities. Though inside it, I had remained at the margins – for the previous year I really hadn't been living in America but in a sort of halfway country, a sort of satellite life outside the life that went on, tenuously linked to the American way of life by work and a common currency, shops and television. Now, though I would always be in a sense apart from it, always be more Nigerian than American, I also had to strive for a place inside it; I had to find a way to be both apart from and part of this vast country.

Thus fortified with resolves (the making of which, you know, dear reader, is the easy part), I wrote to Robo:

'. . . I was really devastated to hear you'd got married. As you can imagine, it's sometimes pretty lonely here and I'd really looked forward to having you over this summer. If I say I understand that we had to break up, I'll be lying. I'm not sure you can ever really understand something like that. So, I don't understand, but I accept. Your husband, whoever he is, is one lucky bastard. I genuinely wish you the best, and whenever I visit Nigeria I hope we can have a drink or lunch or something.

I glowed after I had sent off the letter. I had shown dignity and maturity. My new life had begun on an honourable note.

I called Vivian's place. She answered in a crushed, terrified voice.

'I'm very sorry, Vivian, I'm so ashamed of myself, I'm – '

'Please leave me alone,' Vivian said.

As fast as I could, I blurted out an explanation which I'd made up on the spot – a few days before she called I'd received news from home of the death of a very good friend. I'd been so shocked by the news I didn't sleep for days, and when she called I was suffering from irritability brought on by sleeplessness in addition to my grief for my friend – even then it was no reason to speak to her like that – all I asked for was another chance.

'I'm sorry to hear about your friend,' she said after I had lied passionately for what felt like ten hours. (Well, it wasn't completely a lie, a friend of mine had not died but a fourteen-year old love had, which was nearly as bad.)

'Can I come and see you this weekend?' I asked with incomparable humility.

She didn't say anything.

'Five p.m., Saturday?' I said.

'OK,' she said in a tiny voice.

I put the phone down and smiled broadly. There's nothing in this world as wonderful as a kind-hearted woman.

I went to visit my Uncle Happiness (whom I hadn't seen since Ezendu's party for the politician Prime) partly because I wanted to share with him the goodwill that had begun to ooze out of me after I made my post-Robo resolves, and partly because I would need his help in getting a green card. I hadn't earned any money in a long time, but I shelled out for a bottle of Piper Sonoma and a Heineken six-pack.

Happiness's living room smelt even worse than I remembered it from the previous year. You would think a rat had died and was rotting away in a corner of the room. After letting me in, he sank into a corner of his massive ragged sofa. He had aged terribly, the skin on his chin was wrinkled and sagging like a scrotal sac; there were cuts on his lip which gave his mouth the appearance of chipped china.

'How are you?' I asked.

'I'm not fine,' he said shortly.

'Are you sick?'

'Yes, I am sick. I work too hard. My back is paining me. I started my music business hoping that when it stabilised I would stop doing all these lousy jobs that are not good for the health, but Ezendu ruined my business. He went about telling people that I was a drunkard, that I spoilt his party for the important white politician, when all I wanted was to make the place lively. So now I have to do all these lousy jobs. I'm sick.'

'I'm sorry to hear that, Uncle. I came to thank you for all your help when I first got here. I brought you some drinks.'

Happiness perked up. 'What help? When I couldn't even provide a room for you because of those ingrates who were staying in my house? You know, I threw them out early this year, all of them. Useless people.'

I took the drinks out of the shopping bags and placed them on the stool in front of him. The smile on his face broadened, the bitter, depressed Happiness I saw earlier had vanished.

'My son,' he said, 'you have done well. I did not expect, and I know I do not deserve, but since you have thought me deserving, God will bless you. If I had lived my life like a sensible person, you would not have had any problems when you got to this country. I was supposed to make a way for you and for others who will come after you. I failed, I know I failed, so don't argue with me. Instead of helping you I tried to steal your money. This country turns you into a liar and a thief, or maybe we are all already liars and thieves and this country just provides us with many opportunities to do those things. But if I spend my life cursing myself for all the things I have done wrong, it won't change anything, so no matter what happens I try to be happy. That's the meaning of my name: Happiness.'

Happiness examined the label on the bottle of sparkling wine. 'Our ancestors,' he said, 'usually drink dry gin, but they'll have to make do with California wine this evening.'

He chuckled and poured libation on the tired, old carpet.

'We pray for good health. We have come to this land, past a great sea, in search of prosperity. We pray that we find it in abundance. Even if we all can't find prosperity, let those who can't find riches at least enjoy good health. We know we can't all be wealthy, otherwise on whose heads will the wealthy piss? Who will sing the praises of those who are rich if we are all rich? So we pray for wealth for some and good health for those who do not have the energy to wrestle with prosperity.'

He sprinkled some more wine on the carpet. 'We pray for protection in this country, protection from evil people and from bills. Even if you can barely find food to eat, the bills will pursue you every month in small envelopes; even when you are sick and dying, they will keep following you. Those small envelopes will even follow you into your grave. So we pray for protection so that bills will not kill us before our time.'

He chuckled again and sprinkled more libation. 'We pray for our country. Some people say it is a land of no hope, that we should not waste our strength hoping it will get better. But the lame have been known to walk, the blind have been known to see, even the dead have risen again, so we will not lose hope. We will keep praying for our land. Even if it never gets better, let it not get worse. Our people say: if I do not grow fatter, please let me not grow thinner either. So let it be with our country. All these we ask of our ancestors and also of our Lord Jesus Christ.'

I told my uncle he had prayed a good prayer. He thanked me, filled a glass and gulped the wine down. He re-filled his glass and gulped down half of it before putting the glass back on the stool. Then he poured some for me.

'How is your mother?' he asked.

'She's very well, I speak to them often.'

'She's a good and hard-working woman,' Happiness said. 'A good and hard-working woman.' He lowered his head, stared into his glass of sparkling wine, 'The only problem with her is that she doesn't understand why everyone in the world cannot be as good and hard-working as she is.'

He stood up suddenly. 'This place is so quiet, as if someone has died, and this the house of a music-maker. This is a day for celebration. My son has come to see me, has brought me wine. Who can be happier than Happiness on a day like this?'

He half-ran to the room-divider, stacked with ancient cassette decks, amplifiers and stabilisers, and fiddled with several pieces of equipment until the *highlife* tune *Sweet Mother* began to croak out of the loudspeakers at the four corners of the room.

200

Uncle Happiness was returning to his seat when it seemed as though an invisible something slapped his face. He stopped, frowning, rubbed his cheek for a long moment, then he looked left, looked right and took off on a trot towards the far end of the living room. He stopped just short of the wall and swung round, a big grin on his face. He took off again, missed my seat by inches, then stopped just short of the wall again and swung round. His boomerang legs curved so deeply a car would have driven through the hollow between them, he began to rock back and forth vigorously like a boat caught in turbulent waters.

'Get up, my son, get up and dance,' Uncle Happiness yelled at me. 'Why do you sit there like someone with broken legs? Dancing is in your blood. My grandfather, your great-grandfather, died dancing at a funeral. They say he danced so well the crowd would not let him return to his seat, and he was already an old man, so he danced and danced until he fell down and died. Yes, you have dancing in your blood, so why are you letting this beautiful music go to waste?'